Wow, so this is what it feels like to get punched in the face.

The thought barely finished crossing Val's mind when a boot buried itself in her stomach. She gagged, curling up on her side. From above her, came rage filled obscenities and spit that rained down on her face.

"Bitch! Fucking bitch, fucking with my man." The girl was seething. "You and your fucking slut of a sister..."

Her diatribe faded away as she blasted her fist into Val's face again. Val cried out as her head snapped back. Scrambling, she struggled to push herself to her feet but her balance was shot as she was shoved and kicked back down to the floor like a dog.

"Stop it! Stop!" she tried to say, tried to get her hands up to push the girl away.

This crazy girl who she didn't even *know*!

But the girl came at her ferociously. She dodged and weaved, moving past Val's poor, breathless defenses and grabbed two tight fistfuls of her hair. Val howled in pain, deliriously wondering when mall security was going to show up. She cried out again as her head was wrenched forward then shoved back, connecting with the floor.

The world echoed, faded, then went dark.

When you're caught in a traffic jam, you've got nowhere to go...

Val Delton's life is spiraling and there's nothing she can do to stop it. Her dad lost his job, her mom works fourteen hour days to pay the bills and yet somehow there are high-end shopping bags and an iPod in her older sister's room. Naturally, Val becomes suspicious but her sister's lips are sealed. Then by accident, she uncovers a dark, dangerous secret hidden behind her sister's bright smiles and cool indifference. Val has no idea how far and how deep the repercussions of her sister's secret will reach but she'll do whatever it takes to keep her family safe. Will she succeed before her sister's secret destroys everyone she loves?

Kudos for *TRAFFIC JAM*

Traffic Jam by Melissa Groeling is a smart, sassy, and contemporary YA novel. Our heroine Val is a sophomore in high school. She is a shy, troubled girl with more than her share of problems who longs to be as popular as her older sister Samantha. With her father out of work and her mother working ungodly long hours to pay the bills, Val and her siblings are suffering from the fallout. But when Val discovers expensive items in her sister's room that she knows Sam can't afford to buy, Val's problems get much, much worse...It is the kind of book you can curl up with on a rainy afternoon, with a hot cup of tea and a nice fire in the fireplace, and escape back to a time when homework and a desire for the smoking-hot boy next door seemed to be your biggest problems—until you found out what the world is really like. – *Taylor, reviewer*

Since I absolutely hated high school, Traffic Jam by Melissa Groeling had two strikes against it before I even started it. But I was quite surprised to find I enjoyed it. While it is a YA book that will actually appeal more to young adults than older ones, it is a well-written and accurate depiction of the life of young sophomore in high school. Groeling has a good feel for the mind of her character and the book had a strong ring of truth...Traffic Jam is the story of one young girl's journey through a pivotal year of her life, a story of young love and of finding the courage to do whatever it takes to keep those you love safe. All in all, it is a marvelous piece of work. – *Regan, reviewer*

TRAFFIC

JAM

By

MELISSA GROELING

A BLACK OPAL BOOKS PUBLICATION

GENRE: YA/SUSPENSE

First Publication: MAY 2012

Published by Black Opal Books http://www.blackopalbooks.com

DEDICATION

For Mom and Dad who save me every day of my life.

Thanks to Joe Onorato for his astounding talent on this book cover!

And of course thanks to everyone at Black Opal Books and beyond for all their support!

Michelle + Joey —
Thank you so much!
I also hope you enjoy it!
Melissa
Groeling
:)

CHAPTER 1

C hoke up on the bat, Val! Choke up!"

Val Delton sighed at the command and inched her hands upwards on the baseball bat. She'd forgotten her batting gloves yet again, and she could feel a blister forming on the side of her thumb.

It was the bottom of the ninth and just getting there had been like a double period of history with Mr. Asnor droning on and on about the Greeks and the Romans. He was quite possibly the only person on Earth who could make *Gladiator* sound like the most boring movie ever made. As it stood now, Val would take that double period over this game any day of the week. It was seriously the longest game *ever*. The sun had been up when the game started but now night had completely fallen, the stars blotted out by the field lights.

She heaved another sigh, thinking about the twenty-question assignment she still had to do for biology. How was she even supposed to hold a pen when there was a blister the size of a golf ball on her finger? She doubted Dr. Bennington would see that as a valid excuse for not doing the work. And then she still had to put the finishing touches on that book report—

The ball whizzed by her face, inches from her nose.

"*Striiiiike!*" the umpire belted out.

Val jumped. "Hey, I wasn't ready!"

"You're ready when you're inside the batter's box," the umpire informed her.

Cheers came from the players out in the field. Rolling her eyes, she stepped *out* of the batter's box and took a few practice swings. The bat felt heavy and useless in her hands and she winced as she chafed her blister against the rubber grip. She scowled to herself. She couldn't believe she let her dad talk her into playing another season. There were clumps of dirt in her socks, dust in her hair, her stirrups were crumpling around her ankles, and the sweat stains under her arms were growing embarrassingly large by the second. Just a few more reasons on a long list of many to quit this stupid league.

"Valerie!" Coach Briello shouted impatiently. "Come on, focus! Eye on the ball, you hear me? *Eye on the ball!*"

It was the same advice he'd been shouting since the game started and judging by the gap in the score—*that would be 19-3, thank you very much*—it wasn't doing much good. It had been three and a half hours chocked full of bad umpire calls, missed grounders, and high-fly balls that couldn't be seen coming down from the sky because the people who built the ball park had Shea Stadium in mind. The towering field lights set the field ablaze like a monstrous bonfire and lit an area with a radius of about twenty square miles as well.

But Coach Briello refused to call a forfeit. He stood outside the dugout with his arms crossed, his chest puffed out, hat pulled down low over his eyes, looking more like a captain at the bow of a warship, just seconds away from ordering his crew to fire the first torpedo. For every umpire call he didn't agree with, he challenged it with the ferocity of an enraged pit bull as if the World Series lay on the line rather than the exhausted efforts of a recreational girls' softball team. In the shadow of the dugout, Val could see her team seated along the bench, bleary eyed and dejected, leaning against one another as if to keep each other from pitching face first into the dirt.

"Look alive!" Coach Briello roared.

Val shuffled back up to home plate. She hoisted the bat over her shoulder.

"Full count!" the catcher yelled. "Come on, Diane! Strike her out!"

Yeah, strike me out so we can all be put out of our misery, Val thought.

She glanced down at the catcher and she could see Becca's blue eyes twinkling up at her through her mask.

"What's up, Val?" she smirked.

"Hey," Val muttered.

She turned her attention towards Diane, who was winding up a pitch. Val had a moment to think that Diane shouldn't even be playing recreational softball. The girl had an arm that could take the bark off of a tree. Val had heard once that she actually knocked an umpire out cold when one of her pitches went wild. Rumor or not, it was still enough to invoke a healthy amount of fear.

With a strange mix of fascination and terror, Val watched as Diane pinwheeled her arm and sent the ball streaking towards her. She scrunched her eyes shut and swung.

Craaaack!

The thick vibration of the bat hitting the ball sent a tremor down the bat and into her hands. Her eyes flew open and she watched, mesmerized, as the ball floated like a miniature moon against the dark backdrop of the sky, as if suspended there by a string. Then the ball was sailing in a hard curve into right field.

Val gaped.

Cheers and shouts came from her teammates and more came from the bleachers, jarring her from her stupor. She dropped the bat. Excitement and adrenaline boiled in her gut as she broke out into a frenzied run towards first base.

Oh my God, I hit it! Oh my God! I hit a ball going the speed of sound!

She thought she was flying, her cleats barely touching the ground as she rounded towards second. Man, she didn't even run this fast when she was late for school. Her heart thudded in her ears. She wanted to look over her shoulder to see where the ball was but she was afraid she'd trip and do a magnificent face-plant. Tucking her elbows into her sides, she launched herself towards third.

Dude, stop! Go back! You won't make it! What're you doing?

But her legs seemed determined to carry her farther. As if through an echoing tunnel, she could hear people hollering and yelling.

"She's going for third!"

"Come on! Go! Go! Go!"

"Keep going!"

The cheers around her reached a pitch of urgency and she knew that the ball was close.

Close. God, it was gonna be close...

If she had any air, she'd scream.

"Slide! Slide!" someone exclaimed.

From beneath the rim of her helmet and with sweat stinging her eyes, she saw the third baseman's glove come up. Sucking in a deep breath, she threw herself into the dirt like a human javelin. She slid like a fish in water, eyes tearing up, dirt and dust shooting up her nose and into her mouth. Her outstretched hands touched the base, and she came to a halt, almost over sliding. Billowing brown clouds rose around her like fog. A split second later there was a muffled *thwump* as the ball slammed into the baseman's glove.

Her ears popped. For a second, she lay still, too afraid to move. She clutched at the base like a life preserver. Then slowly, she stood and applause erupted around her. Blinking dust from her eyes, she saw her coach bouncing around like a half-mad Mexican Jumping Bean. Her teammates were going crazy.

"Yeah! Way to hustle!"

"Good job!"

"That's what I want to see!"

"Way to go, Valerie!"

"Good slide, Val!" Coach Briello cried, pumping his fist into the air.

Val broke out in shaky laughter, unable to believe what had just happened. She wiped the sweat from her face.

There's no way Mom and Dad are gonna believe that I hit a triple! Not even Sam's gonna believe it! Neither will Justin!

There was a hard poke at her shoulder. She turned to find herself face-to-face with the umpire.

"You're out," he said.

The smile froze on her face. "What?"

"You're out."

She blinked. "I—"

"What'd you say, ump?" Coach Briello cut in, rushing over like a small swirling thunderstorm.

Val shook her head, frowning. "No, I'm not."

"What?" came from the dugout.

"How is she out?"

"Is he blind or what?"

"You're the last out. Game's over," the umpire said with finality.

"But I got here before the ball did," Val insisted. "I heard it."

"You heard wrong."

"How exactly is she out, ump?" Coach Briello barked. "She made it safely to the base. I *saw* it with my own eyes."

There was a commotion behind Val. She looked over her shoulder to see the other team high-fiving and congratulating each other. It felt like someone had dumped ice over her head.

"I heard the ball hit her glove after I got to the base," she tried again. "I know I did."

"Sorry," the umpire said even though his tone wasn't the least bit apologetic. "From where I stood, she tagged you."

Val stared at him, the surge of adrenaline for hitting a triple now cooling off to the shoulder-sagging misery of striking out. Her team groaned and grumbled in disappointment.

Coach Briello, however, was not about to go down quietly. "This is ridiculous!" he bellowed, his thin black moustache trembling. "I have had it up to *here* with you, ump! You've been making bad calls throughout this entire game and my team and I have suffered for it. She was safe, you hear me? I was watching from right over there!"

"Hey, that's the way I saw it," the umpire snapped. "You don't have to like it but that's the way it happened, all right?"

"This game is not played by cheating!" Coach Briello ranted angrily.

Val glared at the umpire, wishing she could see his face through his mask. She yanked off her helmet. It was no use, really. Once Coach Briello started yelling, it only made the umpires stick more firmly to their calls, whether they were bad or not.

"That's the way I saw it. If you don't like it, you can request to have another umpire call your games."

"I don't want another umpire!" Coach Briello shot back. "I want you to admit your mistake. She was safe!"

"I'm not going to admit anything. She's out. End of story."

Val turned on her heel and stomped into the dugout. Sure, she didn't want to play this stupid sport anymore but *God*, her first triple and it ended with her being called out because the umpire was an absolute moron. Make that a *blind* moron.

"Oh no! No, we are not done yet!" Coach Briello shouted after her. "Valerie, get your helmet back on! We are continuing this game immediately!"

"Coach, this game is over," the umpire insisted. "It's the bottom of the ninth and she was the last out."

"Like hell!" he cried, flailing his arms like an acrobat teetering on a high wire.

The umpire walked away from him. Coach Briello followed like an irate puppy nipping at his heels.

Val tossed her helmet to the ground and sank onto the dugout bench with a miserable groan. "Well that sucked."

"It was a good hit, Val," Keri Anne said, as she took a seat next to her.

Melissa smiled as she sat down on the other side of her. She passed Val a small cup of water. "Textbook slide, too."

Val shrugged. "Would've been better if I was safe."

"Kenny's an idiot. No one can help that."

Val gulped down the water. "Kenny?"

"Yeah. You know, the umpire?"

"*That* was Kenny?"

Keri Anne rolled her brown eyes. She was a tall gangly girl with thick brown hair a face full of freckles. "Who else could call a game this badly?"

"Don't you work with him on the school paper?" Melissa asked.

She was as short as Keri Anne was tall, with olive-colored skin and thick, dark hair that always looked like it belonged in one of those *Pantene* commercials. Val scowled, both at Melissa's enviable hair and Kenny's far-reaching stupidity.

"Yeah. He's a moron there, too."

"Well, at least he's consistent," Keri Anne said with a shrug.

"Consistently lame maybe," Melissa sneered as she shook her hair loose from her ponytail.

"Not to mention blind," Val mumbled.

"Think he has a date for the dance yet?" Melissa wondered.

Keri Anne popped two pieces of gum into her mouth, chewing noisily. "If he does, I feel sorry for her already."

"Whoever he does drag along probably won't be from our high school."

"Is Jim taking you to his senior prom?" Val asked.

Melissa flipped her hair over her shoulder, flashing a satisfied smile. "Of course. I'll probably be the only sophomore there."

Keri Anne gave her a bored look. "Is he coming to our sophomore dance then?"

Melissa's eyes clouded a bit. "No. He thinks it's too...juvenile."

"Hey," Val said, offended.

Keri Anne arched an eyebrow. "He used to be a sophomore once."

Melissa waved a dismissive hand at them. "It doesn't matter. Besides, my parents won't pay for two dresses."

Keri Anne nudged Val with her elbow. "How about you, Val? You going with anyone?"

Melissa snorted softly under her breath before Val could reply. Surprised, Val looked over at her with raised eyebrows.

"What?"

"Yeah, Val, *are* you going with anyone?"

There was a thick layer of *snob* in her tone, and she fixed Val with such a knowing look, Val wondered if she'd been taking lessons from Sam. Sam looked at her that way all the time—sly and amused, like she was waiting for the punch line of a particularly raunchy joke. Except the joke was Val. She felt the skin on the back of her neck prickle.

I am not that pathetic. Am I?

Frowning, she looked down at her cleats. "I'm...Well, I'm not sure if I'm going yet."

She could almost feel Melissa's smirk. "That's code for no one's asked you."

Val narrowed her eyes at her. "How do you know?"

Melissa's smirk deepened. "I would've heard otherwise."

Val bit the inside of her cheek. God, she *hated* high school. Didn't anyone have anything better to do than to keep track of everyone else's business?

"Well, there's still time," Keri Anne piped up, trying at least to be nice. "I mean, the dance is like two months away still."

"It takes two months just to pick out a dress," Melissa sniffed.

Keri Anne rolled her eyes. "It does not."

"It does too," Melissa insisted with authority. "I remember Jim taking me to his junior prom last year and it took me *forever* to choose a dress and by the time I did, there was barely enough time for the alterations. It was *such* a pain in the ass."

Keri Anne wasn't buying it. "Dude, it takes you two *hours* just to decide what you're going to wear to school every morning."

"It does not."

"Does, too."

"Can I help it if I want to look good?"

"Looking good is one thing. Getting detention every day for being late because of it is something else."

Melissa laughed. "You should've heard my bio teacher when I told him I was late because I was getting a manicure."

Keri Anne chuckled. "You're ridiculous."

"Hey, these bad boys are awesome." She held up her hands, splaying her fingers. As if to make up for the fact that her hands were as small as the rest of her, Melissa's fingernails were ferociously long and painted a deep teal color with silver sparkly lines spaced across each nail like a rainbow.

Keri Anne was eyeing them skeptically. "How do you even put your softball glove on?"

"Very carefully."

"How often do they break off?"

"Quite often actually. I keep that nail salon in business."

"And it's never crossed your mind that you might be blowing your money away?"

"It's not my money," she said with a careless shrug. "Jim pays for them. He likes them. A lot. Especially when I—"

"Whoa, whoa, hey, don't need the details." Keri Anne cut her off with a laugh. "Or the images, thank you very much."

Melissa snickered then jabbed Val in the ribs when she saw that she wasn't laughing.

"Don't be such a prude."

"I didn't say anything."

"No, but you're looking like you just swallowed a bug."

Val tried to school her expression into something more pleasant. "No, I'm not—"

"Maybe if you actually crawled out of the homework hole you like to dig for yourself every weekend, you'd—"

"I do *not* have a homework hole," Val said indignantly, her cheeks turning red when Keri Anne tried to stifle her laughter. "I just...I'm just busy."

"Oh come *on*. Busy doing what? Extra credit that you don't need?" Melissa rolled her eyes. "You've already got straight A's. You're set for the rest of the year. It's not going to kill you to come out on a Friday night."

Biting her tongue in frustration, Val dug a small crevice in the dirt with the toe of her cleat. *Great, here it comes. Another round of Let's-State-The-Obvious. As if I want to hang around with a bunch of idiots who do nothing but get stupidly drunk off the nasty beer that someone stole from their dad's stash and then proceed to puke and pass out. Or pass out then puke, whichever comes first.*

"Look, I know things are probably rough with your dad losing his job and all—" Melissa continued.

Seriously why couldn't she just shut up about things she didn't understand?

"—but surely he's allowing you to at least have a life and—"

"My dad lets me go out," Val cut in sharply.

"Then why don't you? And going to the library doesn't count. You've got to *socialize*, Val. It's the only way you're going to get a date for the dance. And you *want* a date for the dance, don't you? You've got to let people know that you're *alive*."

"I'm alive," she said after a pause, hating the way her voice came out meek and uncertain.

Hating the way Melissa laughed at her.

"Why don't you ask your sister for some pointers, Val? I'm sure she can—"

There was an instant burning resentment in Val's chest at the mention of Sam.

"I do *not* need to ask my sister how to have fun."

"Hey, don't get snippy. I'm just trying to help."

"Yeah, you're *so* helpful."

"Well, it's not my fault you can't take good advice."

Val looked away, her jaw clenching and unclenching. Melissa scoffed and stood up.

"Whatever."

She walked away. Without a word, Keri Anne got up and followed her. Val remained where she was, feeling the blood pound in her face, wondering wildly how a conversation about Kenny being a horrible umpire could've morphed into a running commentary on Val's social life or lack thereof. She stared at the ground, listening with half an ear as her teammates moved around her, collecting their gear. She wondered how much of the conversation they'd overheard and if they agreed with Melissa. She heard someone laughing and the embarrassment sank deeper into her bones, keeping her frozen in place. It took her a moment to realize it wasn't only embarrassment that weighed her down. It was the knowledge that Melissa was right.

Val had always been a bit of a loner. She wasn't sure when it actually started—when she decided that dealing with schoolwork was preferable to dealing with people. It was probably around the time her dad lost his job as a construction foreman last year. He'd been at that job for nearly seventeen years. When the economy tanked, his job was one of the millions that dissolved.

They were forced to move from their comfortable, two-story house to a three-bedroom apartment that was right smack in the center of town. It was surprisingly convenient but that fact was overridden daily by how small, loud, and noisy it was. The toilet didn't work fifty percent of the time and there was nowhere to store her mountain bike. Currently it was standing on its back tire, crammed into the hall closet.

So while her dad scrambled to find work and her mom put in long hours at a local bakery, Val threw herself into her schoolwork—taking on extra assignments, book reports, practically running the school paper. Because as long as she was busy, she wouldn't have to think about what her parents were going through. How they looked, hunched over the kitchen table with bills spread out before them like a nightmarish blanket, their faces creased with worry and frustration and their hands raking continuously through their hair, searching, always searching for a solution.

Val had to share a room with her little brother, Justin and Sam—*I'm the oldest so I get my own room*—was more concerned with her social standing at school than whether or not the phone bill could be paid.

Sam.

Not a day went by that Val didn't wonder what freak act of nature made them related. She knew countless people who had siblings, yet they never seemed to suffer from the confusing circumstances of sharing the same mother and father with a complete stranger. The weird connection, that cosmic alignment of the planets that readily assured her that she was part of the same family tree as her parents and Justin, did not exist between her and Sam. And probably never would as long as the two of them were alive and breathing.

Sam existed on another plane of reality, another dimension. She was every younger sister's worst nightmare—tall, blonde, pretty and popular—and Val found life to be much easier if she just stumbled along in Sam's shadow rather than try to avoid it.

Honestly, who wanted to be friends with her when they could be friends with Sam? Sam, who was the life of the party, who was surely going to get a modeling contract after graduation, who could charm any teacher into giving her an A by simply flashing her pearly whites or by giving them a sob story about how her life had changed so drastically, thanks to the plummeting economy. And honestly, her life really had changed but she refused to draw any attention to it unless it could benefit her in some way. Sam, who palled around with just about everyone, making them think that they were her friend, when in actuality, she wasn't friends with anyone except Audrey, John, and Bryan. But that didn't matter because as long as she acknowledged you, you were her friend even if she wasn't yours.

Val supposed she couldn't really be mad at Melissa. As big of a snob as she was, Melissa was only saying things that Val already knew. Of course that didn't make it sting any less but what was she supposed to do? Sit around and worry about it? There was homework to be done. There were softball games to play. So what if her life was consumed by academics? So what if she missed out on parties every weekend or on hanging out with her friends?

Okay, well, only one friend actually, but still. It was nobody's business what she did with her time. Why did people like Melissa always feel like they had to rub her face in the fact that she basically had no life whatsoever?

She sighed, her shoulders sagging. Besides, she'd take a book report over feeling like this any day.

CHAPTER 2

She barely listened as Coach Briello continued to protest the tribulations of inferior umpiring. It was going on nine-thirty. If Val was in bed by midnight, it would be a miracle. If she left the dugout within the next ten minutes, it would be a biblical event. They had a game on Saturday so Coach Briello advised them.

"Show up an hour early so we can practice, all right?"

Everyone moaned.

"Hey, hey," he said over the noise. "If we're going to lose because of bad umpires, at least we'll look good while we're doing it."

With that, they were dismissed.

Val stood slowly, gathering up her glove. Melissa walked by, bumping her shoulder with a smirk.

"See ya, Val."

Val didn't look at her. "See ya."

"Remember the word *fun*, Val so you can look it up when you get home tonight, okay?"

Val turned bright red as some of her teammates laughed. She put her glove down on the bench and squatted down, pretending to tie her cleats. Her fingers shook and she kept her head down as everyone fled the dugout.

"Sacrificing your body for the game, huh?"

Startled, Val looked up.

Her friend—well, her only friend, Allison, stood smiling down at her from the other side of the chain link fence that made up the back wall of the dugout. The sight of her relaxed the knot that had formed in the center of Val's back. Allison, she knew, would never give her crap about her study habits or her lack of a life or anything else for that matter. Unless Val asked and even then, Allison would give her one of her searching looks and say, *does it really matter?*

Val smiled, straightening. "You saw?"

"Sure did. Pretty nice moves there, Jeter."

Val laughed. "Yeah and then I got called out."

Allison shook her head, her long blonde hair sliding over her shoulders as she moved. "Kenny's a jackass."

"How did everyone but me know that he was umping tonight's game?"

"You didn't get the memo?"

"Must've missed it."

"Again?"

"Again. So where're you headed?" Val asked, leaning a shoulder against the fence.

"J.R.'s having a party. Want to come along?"

Val glanced down at her sweat-stained uniform. "Not exactly dressed for it and I thought you two broke up."

Allison's green eyes flicked away then came back, sheepishly. "We talked." Val raised an eyebrow, unimpressed. Allison shrugged, the small diamond stud in her nose twinkling softly. "He seemed pretty sorry."

"You believe him?"

Allison shrugged again. Val looked at her, not saying anything.

"I know, I know, *I know*," Allison relented. "I just—I don't know, Val. It's like, I can never say no to him, and he was down on his knees and everything."

"Was he proposing?"

"No, smartass, he wasn't. He apologized and...well—"

"Yeah."

It took a lot for Val not to let any judgment color her tone. She was the last person to be giving out relationship advice seeing as how she had no experience to speak of, but Allison was her friend and J.R. never ceased being a jackass.

"This is the third time you caught him cheating on you," Val reminded her gently.

Allison let out a long breath. Her fingers played with the edges of the fence, her brow furrowed. Val almost wished she knew what her friend was going through so that she could understand, so that maybe she could bestow some great words of wisdom upon her. But if she had to deal with a guy like J.R., Val was sure her head would explode.

"We'll see how things go at the party," Allison finally said but her eyes were troubled.

"You don't have to go, you know," Val said. "To the party, I mean."

"I told him I'd be there."

"Tell him you got clobbered in the head by a baseball and had to go to the hospital because of a concussion."

The corners of her mouth twitched. "You sound like you've used that one before."

"Actually I heard Sam use it once to get out of a date with Mark."

The second the words were out of her mouth, she wished she could take them back. It was like a tic she couldn't control. As much as she hated it when anyone else brought up Sam, she found herself doing it repeatedly. It made absolutely no sense. But Allison didn't seem to notice.

"Ugh, Mark Colitto?"

"Yeah."

"What did she ever see in him?"

"The same thing she sees in all the other losers she dates."

Allison's chuckle suddenly turned sly. "And speaking of your sister—"

"Uh oh."

"It's not bad," she paused. "Well, depending on how you look at it."

Val braced herself. "Please tell me you didn't see her in town. She's supposed to be grounded and if she snuck out again—"

"No, no, no," Allison cut in then stopped. "Wait, she's grounded? Again?"

"Came home too late a few nights ago. Said she lost track of time."

"Again?"

"Again."

"Girl needs a watch."

"One that works, too."

Allison shook her head then said, "Okay, okay, before I forget. I saw a friend of Sam's on the way over here."

Val raised her eyebrows expectantly. Instead of answering, Allison simply stared at her, a slow smile creeping across her face. The sight of it made Val fidget.

"Okay, so you want me to guess or—"

"John."

"God, Allison," Val groaned.

She dropped her head forward until it rested on the fence. A wave of heat crawled up the back of her neck.

"What?" Allison laughed. "I'm just telling you who I saw."

Val sighed then looked over her shoulder. "You know that's how rumors start."

"Yeah but it would be the best *kind* of rumor."

"I didn't know there was a best kind."

"Sure there is. The kind that is so fantastic, *no one* believes it."

"No one but you," Val rolled her eyes.

"And you."

"It's not true anyway."

"Dude, don't even try it," Allison smirked. "Your head's always on the brink of catching fire whenever his name is mentioned."

"That's because he's creepy."

"Oh sure." Allison's eyes sparkled with amusement.

"And he's too quiet," Val insisted, knowing it wouldn't do her much good.

"Uh huh."

"You know it's the quiet ones you've got to watch out for."

"Right."

"Allison, I do *not* like him."

Allison grinned. "Yes, you do. When are you going to stop being in denial?"

Val looked away, picking at the fence with her nail. Allison had been after her for nearly a year to nut up and say something to the guy. Say something, anything, write him a note, sing him a song, wax poetic, *anything* to get Val to finally act on the stars that appeared in her eyes every time John was around. And he was around quite often, being one of Sam's best friends and all, only Val normally spent that time closed up in her room.

The possibility of making an ass out of herself was far too great whenever she heard his low, raspy voice—the sound of it was like a thrumming against her back teeth like a plucked guitar string—so it was safer for her to make herself scarce. And God, if Sam ever found out, Val would never live it down. Not to mention that Sam would make every effort to make sure nothing ever happened—not that anything would happen anyway, but if by some stroke of fate, something was to happen, it would never be given the chance to get off the ground. Sam's friends were hers and hers alone. She did not share.

Val sighed.

"Uh oh, are you getting starry-eyed again?" Allison's amused voice pulled her back from her thoughts.

Val looked at her then at the ground. "It would never work, Allison. Even if I did grow a set."

"You don't know that," she countered, the humor fading from her eyes.

"Yes, I do."

"Why? Because of Sam?"

"Well, duh."

Allison let out a long breath. "She can't ruin your life unless you let her, Val. And John's a big boy. If he ever wanted to see you or whatever, then that's his decision, not hers."

"Yeah, that's a big, fat *if*. And besides, Sam probably won't talk to either one of us ever again."

"She'll get over it."

Val remained skeptical. "I doubt it."

"She will," Allison said firmly. "He's her friend, not a boyfriend or anything, right?"

"I think they hooked up once a long time ago."

"See? Fair game."

Val gave a tired smile. "You make it sound so easy."

"It is. You're just letting your brain get in the way, that's all."

"It's a bad habit."

"Filthy. You need to break it."

"I know."

A car honked and Val looked over to see her mother, waving at her.

"Tell your mom I said hi," Allison said. "And wish me luck at this stupid party."

"You sure you want to go? My mom could give you a ride home."

"Nah, it's okay. I'll see you at school tomorrow."

"Good luck, man."

"See you."

"Bye."

Val watched her go then hurried towards her mother's car. Behind her, the field lights flicked off, one at a time until the field was swallowed up in complete darkness.

CHAPTER 3

Sam! Come on, will you hurry up?"

It was too early for this. Seriously. But nonetheless, Val stood outside the bathroom door, the *locked* bathroom door, in her pajamas, hollering for her take-all-day-long sister to get out of the bathroom so she could at least brush her teeth. She was going to be *late*. The newspaper deadline was today, this morning, and she was going to miss it because Sam's hair was somehow more important than life itself.

"Will you wait? God!" Sam shot back, her voice muffled by the old splintered door.

"You've been in there all morning! How much longer do you need?"

"This is the only room with a half-decent mirror."

"You have a full-length one in your room."

"Dad hasn't hung it up yet."

With a groan, Val thumped her forehead against the door. "Will you *please* just hurry up?"

"What do you need to do in here that's so important?"

"What do you think? It's a *bathroom*."

Val heard her snicker, prompting her to pound on the door again. "Sam, come on!"

"I'm almost done."

"No, you're not—Mom! Sam won't get out of the bathroom!"

Christina Delton, looking like she'd barely slept in two days, came storming down the hallway. Her bright blue eyes flashed with exhaustion and annoyance. The baker's coat she wore over her flour-streaked jeans and T-shirt flared behind her like a cape. Blonde hair was piled on the top of her head in a messy bun. It was she who Sam took after— all milky smooth skin and lean limbs. Val took after their dad—dark and short, needing her brains to get by more than the simple fact of being pretty to look at. Although right now, Mom was far from being pretty. Her face was drawn and lined, evidence of pulling a double shift at the bakery. Val wouldn't be surprised if she'd just gotten home.

"You two, I swear to God, one of these days," Mom exclaimed. "What the hell is going on here?"

"I need to get in the bathroom. Sam's been in there all morning. I'm gonna be late."

"You're not even dressed yet."

"See?" taunted Sam from inside the bathroom.

"I would be able to get dressed if I could get into the bathroom!"

"Get dressed in your room," Sam suggested.

"I am not getting dressed with Justin in there. That's gross and totally inhumane."

"Inhumane for who? Him?"

"Sam—!" Val started to yell.

"Sam!" Mom knocked hard on the door. "You've got five more minutes in there before I have your father break the damn door down, you hear me? Sam?"

"Okay, okay."

Mom turned to Val. "Go and get dressed, Val. She'll be out by the time you're done."

"But—"

"Val, just do it," her mother snapped before walking away.

Val spun back to the room she shared with her brother. She tore through the cardboard boxes that she had yet to unpack, searching savagely for something to wear. Justin sat on the edge of his bed, tying his sneakers.

"You could've just asked me to leave, you know," he said quietly.

Val slowed her search for clothes but didn't look at him. She could feel him watching her, solemnly perched on the crumpled blankets of his bed. His dark brown eyes matched her own. His hair was a blond so light, it was nearly white—not the spun gold of their mom's and Sam's.

In most ways, he was a typical eleven-year-old, in love with his video games, baseball cards and, of course, *Star Wars*. But in other ways, he was not so typical. There was something calm about him. He didn't possess the same frantic work ethic that Val had or the same rebellious streak that drove Sam into being grounded every other weekend. It was a weird thing, Val thought, for a kid to be, but she didn't want to admit that it also came in handy sometimes. Even at his age, Justin could be the small voice of reason, so matter-of-fact that he could divert an argument or curb someone's anger by muttering a few simple words. Sam had taken to calling him "Little Buddha," which always made him laugh.

"Yeah, Justin, I know," she mumbled.

He picked his way around boxes and toys and left the room, closing the door behind him. Val's hands stopped riffling through her clothes and she stared after him. She knew the move had hit him hard. She knew that the manic struggle of day-to-day life probably made him feel like he was lost in the shuffle. God knows, that was how it made her feel. She'd been tempted to try and talk to him about it but she wasn't sure if she should. He hid everything so well behind a mask of calm that she had no idea what bothered him. She shook her head and resumed her search. She had a newspaper deadline to worry about and if Sam was finally done—

"All right, your Royal Highness, the bathroom's all yours."

Val looked up as her bedroom door was flung open and Sam stood in the doorway, eying her reproachfully.

"Do you know how to knock?" she snapped.

"Oh look, you're not even dressed yet. How surprising." Sam rolled her eyes and came into the room, moving through it the same way she moved through everything else, fluid and untouchable, more like an ice queen than a seventeen-year-old pain in Val's ass.

Val gritted her teeth, feeling like her privacy was being invaded. Strangely enough, she never felt that way when Justin was in the room.

Only Sam.

Her blonde hair was cut in a stylishly long shag, streaked with dark purple highlights, done perfectly straight and shining like an oil slick on top of her head. Her makeup, heavy emphasis around her ice-blue eyes and pale around her full, pouty lips, was smooth and natural looking. High cheekbones, slim nose, perfectly-shaped eyebrows— Val wondered if Sam was hiding a stylist in the bathroom closet. Already dressed in tight blue jeans and a white shirt that was only a shade darker than her skin, Sam seemed ready to hit the bricks, but of course, a daily poke-and-laugh at Val was in order.

She watched in silent frustration as Sam peered into the box Val had been rummaging through.

"Well," she said with a smirk. "No wonder you're not dressed yet. Look at all these *fabulous* wardrobe choices."

"I would be dressed if you hadn't barged in here."

Ignoring her, Sam pulled a blue hooded sweatshirt out of the box. She shook it out and held it up, eying it too critically to be serious.

"You get this in the men's department?"

Val snatched it away from her. "Is there a reason why you're in here?"

"Okay, okay, geez, take it easy," Sam said, holding her hands up in surrender. "What crawled up your butt this morning?"

"You," Val started to say but Sam was already talking over her.

"So I heard you hit a triple the other night. Too bad I missed it."

Val gave her a skeptical look. "You never come to my games."

"Well, no, but I would've liked to have seen it though. Just to believe it," she added with a grating smile.

"*You* never hit a triple."

"I don't even play anymore so who cares? I don't know why you're still playing though. You don't even like it."

"It's not bad."

"All you do is complain every time there's a game."

"I do not."

"Yes, you do. What, did Dad talk you into playing another season?"

Val paused. "Maybe."

Sam laughed. "Of course he did. Sucker."

"Well, it's better than being grounded all the time."

Sam rolled her eyes. "I'm not grounded all the time."

"Yes, you are."

"Mom and Dad don't know how to lay off."

"So it's their fault?" Val demanded incredulously as she threw the sweatshirt on her bed.

"Don't start with me, Val. I get enough shit from them."

"Hey, you came into my room."

"So that gives you the moral high ground?"

"Yes, it does."

"God, you are so stup—"

"Sam!" Mom suddenly called from out in the living room. "John's here!"

Val felt her heart thud hard in her chest. *Oh, God. I'm still in my pajamas*!

Rolling her eyes one last time at her younger sister, Sam left the room in a whirl of scented hair products and perfume. Val dove for the door, slamming it shut behind her. She leaned against it, the aggravation of dealing with Sam quickly overpowered by the sheer mortification if John saw her in her pajamas. Pajamas that had *monkeys* on them!

She quickly got dressed, throwing on jeans and a simple purple shirt that had a big cupcake on the front. Running a brush through her hair, she stopped when she caught sight of her reflection in the mirror that hung above the bureau. Melissa's words echoed through her head.

'*You do want a date for the dance, don't you*?'

Val frowned and stared at herself. Okay, so if she was honest, she'd say that *maybe* there were some similarities between herself and Sam. But she was only going to admit one thing and one thing only. They shared the same pale skin and *that was it*. On Sam, it went well with her coloring but on Val, it made her look like she was half-dead. Her hair was a brown so dark, it was almost black and her eyes were just like pots of ink. Her eyelashes were thick and long, making it seem like she wore eyeliner but the truth was she didn't even *own* any makeup. She tried it once, when she was sure she wasn't going to be interrupted for four or five hours and she ended up poking herself in the eye *twice* with an eyeliner pencil and the liquid cover-up she'd used made her break out in a rash.

All in all, a complete and total disaster.

The only thing she ever put on her lips was Chapstick—and her hair, she didn't even know where to begin with that. It didn't flow and cascade like most girls' hair. It just kind of sat there, like a movie prop around her face. It was long, chopped into layers, and a little ways past her shoulders, but unless she fried the hell out of it with a flat-iron, it looked like it hadn't seen a brush in weeks. So she mainly tied it back in a ponytail, or if she was feeling particularly fancy, she'd tie it into a loose braid.

She snarled at her reflection and left the room. Beauty and fashion would just have to wait.

She went down the hallway, her step slowing as she listened for John's voice. All was quiet. She didn't even hear Sam which meant that they already left. She found herself sighing with relief, her stomach untying. *Sorry, Allison*, she thought to herself. *Chickened out yet again.*

She headed into the kitchen and snagged a package of Pop-Tarts. She heated them up in the toaster and got her books together. Slinging her book bag over her shoulder, she put the Pop-Tarts—frosted strawberry, thank you very much—on a napkin and headed out, shutting the door behind her.

"—forgot my lip gloss."

She bit into her Pop-Tart just as she registered Sam's voice behind her. Startled, she turned around to see her sister coming towards her.

Following her was John.

The piece of Pop-Tart lodged itself in her throat.

"Be right back," Sam called to John as she brushed past Val without a word and disappeared into the apartment.

The door closed with a definite *click*, leaving Val out in the hallway with John.

Alone.

Oh God.

She began to have heart palpitations, and they were hard enough to dislodge the piece of Pop-Tart from her throat, allowing her to answer with a squeaked, "hey" when John said, "What's up, Val?"

God, his voice. It was like hot fudge straight out of the bottle. She couldn't find the will to bring her eyes from the floor, knowing what she would find when and if she ever did. She knew because she'd stared at him often enough. She always wondered if he could feel her watching him, like in those trashy romance novels where the woman somehow *feels* the eyes of her man watching her, assessing her and she would feel it like heat trickling over her skin.

Lame. If he could feel you watching him, he'd probably run screaming in the other direction.

Slowly, as if she were submerged in water, she raised her eyes, almost hearing the muscles in her neck creak in protest, taking him in from toe to head and feeling herself pale pathetically beneath the intense stare of his pale green eyes.

She felt caught, like she was doing something she wasn't supposed to, which was silly because he stood there, with his hands in the pockets of his jeans, as quiet and civil as he ever was. But there was something else that always lingered. Something fierce that rolled and rippled beneath the surface. It was something she didn't have a name for. It was something that was just beyond her fingertips, just out of the corner of her eye.

As usual, he had a dark blue bandana around his forehead, pulled down low over his eyes and a large football jersey over his bulky frame. Baggy jeans were low enough so that with his hands in his pockets, his arms were perfectly straight. She was *not* going to think about the boxer shorts that were probably peeking out above his belt too.

Too late.

She was already blushing and she thought she saw his mouth twist into a faint smile.

Oh God please, let me melt into the floor.

"What's for breakfast?" he rasped.

Val's head began to buzz, like a drone of bees decided to take up residence inside her cranium.

Say something! cried a tiny voice. *He's talking to you. Say something! Anything. Come on!*

"Uh—"

Sam reappeared. "Okay, got it. Let's go."

She gave Val an annoyed look then walked off down the hallway. John looked down at her and this time she wasn't hallucinating when she saw his lips pull into a smile. But it was so fleeting, just barely there, not nearly long enough for her brain to store it away for further perusal.

"See ya," he said, his voice grating her eardrums as he followed Sam down the hall.

Val stared after him. The piece of Pop-Tart that was still in her mouth now tasted like dust. She had a horrible feeling that she just blew it.

CHAPTER 4

I can't believe I did that!" Val wailed at lunch. "He was right in front of me and I just—I just froze!"

Allison gave a sympathetic shake of her head although she seemed to be trying awfully hard not to laugh.

"You didn't say *anything?*"

Val looked up from where she'd slammed her head down on top of her folded arms. She was sitting across from her friend in the cafeteria. It was fifth period. The day was just about half over and that was just fine because all Val wanted to do was go home and hide in a corner.

"Yeah. I said 'hey' and 'uh.'"

Allison gave up, snorting laughter into her chocolate milk. "Well, that's two more words than what you've said to him since the last time you saw him."

"Oh my God, you are *so* not helping."

"Come on, you're getting there. Last week was a wave. So at least this way, things have gone verbal and verbal is good."

Val put her head back down with a groan. The smell of her soggy cheeseburger was making her sick and the nonstop chatter, clattering of forks, spoons, knives, people slurping, chewing, tearing, drinking—it was enough to make her want to barf.

"It's not that bad," Allison insisted.

"Yes, it is," Val said, her voice muffled.

"Can't hear you when you're talking to the table, dude."

She groggily picked her head back up. "It is that bad. He probably thinks I'm mental or something."

"Baby steps, Val. Baby steps."

"He's been a friend of Sam's for, like, ever. He's been over for dinner on more than one occasion. I should be *able* to say more than just 'hey' and 'uh' to him. This is so pathetic. *I* am so pathetic!"

"Will you give yourself a break before someone tosses you into a padded room? Hot guys are supposed to be scary."

"I'm not scared of him."

Allison raised an eyebrow. "You're scared of something."

Val raised an eyebrow right back at her. "If I can face down Diane on a softball field, I should be able to—"

A lunch tray plunked down next to hers. "Did someone say softball?"

Val and Allison looked up to see Kenny standing next to their table. They groaned in unison.

"Kenny, go be annoying somewhere else," Allison said.

"Yes, please," Val agreed.

But trying to insult Kenny was like asking fire not to burn. It was impossible. *He* was impossible, both in school and on the field and everywhere else in between.

"Nah, I think this seat will suit me just fine." He dropped into the empty seat next to Val, making sure to bump her shoulder several times as he made himself comfortable.

"Ugh, my God, do you mind?" Val snapped.

"Nope." His light blue eyes twinkled with the smugness and eagerness of a hungry, salivating hyena. He always seemed to believe that when people didn't want him around, that meant there was some kind of secret to be sniffed out. "Article potential" is what he called it for the school newspaper. The word *privacy* held no meaning to him whatsoever.

His tanned face was chiseled and rough from too many hours outside playing baseball. Blonde hair was constantly hidden beneath a dirty white baseball hat that was turned backwards. His jeans and flannel shirt—two things that he obviously had an abundance of because no one has ever seen him in anything else beside his baseball uniform— looked like they'd been slept in. Honestly, Val had never known a jock with the ability to string two sentences together and Kenny was no exception, which is why she couldn't understand how or why he was even on the school paper.

Val glared at him. "What do you want?"

"Oh, I was just walking by and it seemed you were having some kind of a breakdown. Thought I'd come over and offer my services."

"Services of what, man, being a pain-in-the-ass?" she asked.

Allison snickered.

Kenny popped open his carton of milk. "You see?" he said after he'd taken a large swallow. "This is exactly why you never win your softball games."

"What?"

"Your attitude."

"My attitude on the field might have something to do with the fact that you can't call a fair game."

Kenny gave an exaggerated eye-roll.

"Don't even, Kenny," Allison said. "I know that and I don't even play softball."

"You don't know what you're missing," Kenny replied. "So listen, Val. What's the problem? Anything I can help you with?"

"No."

"You sure?"

"Yes."

He turned to Allison who shook her head at him. "Like I'm going to say anything to you?"

Kenny pretended to be hurt. "Why not?"

"Because anything anyone ever says to you ends up in the paper."

"Only the important stuff."

"Important or not, it still ends up in the paper."

"Like I said, it's *important*."

Val sighed in aggravation. "Kenny, whether or not the quarterback is cheating on Melissa is not important and furthermore, it's none of anyone's business."

"Yeah, but it made me awfully popular."

"Dude, the whole football team came after you," Allison pointed out.

Kenny laughed. "And it was awesome, especially since half of them can't run nearly as fast as I can."

Val was not amused. "The paper is just that. A paper. It's not for trash."

Kenny's eyes suddenly narrowed on her face. "My articles are not trash."

"I'm not saying your articles are trash. I'm saying—"

"Then what? What're you saying? That you can write better than me? That your articles are somehow better than mine?" His voice rose and the humor was gone from his face so fast it was like someone had wiped it clean with a dish rag. People around them stopped to stare.

"Geez, Kenny, calm down," Allison said.

Kenny ignored her. His eyes shot icy daggers at Val, who was stunned at his reaction. She'd never seen him anywhere outside of smug, irritating and cocky. Now here he was looking like he was seconds away from wringing her neck. She pressed her lips together, suddenly too aware of the attention they were receiving. She shifted uncomfortably in her seat.

"I wasn't—" she tried to say but Kenny cut her off again, getting in her face.

"What? Huh? You weren't what? Come on, dazzle me since you think you're *so* much better than me."

"I never said that," she exclaimed, a strange kind of numbness coming over her.

"Kenny," Allison snapped from across the table. "Back off."

"Shut your face, Allison," he shot back.

"Don't tell me to shut my face, jackass. You're the one who sat down at this table. You can always eat somewhere else."

"And you can always shut the hell up. This has nothing to do with you."

"Oh, please," she scoffed. "This? This right here? What exactly is this? Val calling it like it is? You're surprised? Everyone knows the crap you write about is just that. Crap. I don't know why you're getting so pissed off."

Kenny's face was turning an alarming shade of red. Val mentally scrambled for something that would stop this from going any further but she remained frozen to her seat, unable to speak or move.

"You are a bitch," Kenny hissed at Allison, the veins in his neck straining. "No wonder J.R.'s cheating on you."

Allison went white.

Kenny turned to Val as he stood up. "There. How about that, Val? That trashy enough for you?"

He stalked away.

Val gaped after him, her cheeks burning. Murmurs of laughter and "oh my God, did you just hear what he said?" rose up around them, coming in from all sides, crushing against her and she sucked in a painful breath before looking over at her friend. Allison stared motionless down at her tray. Her face was pale, freckles standing out like spots of ink. Her hands were clenched tightly on the table.

"Allison," Val said quietly. "I'm—"

Allison got to her feet without a word and left the cafeteria. Val watched her go, her eyes beginning to burn. She didn't move until the bell rang.

CHAPTER 5

After school, she walked home with guilt weighing down her every step. *I should've stepped in. I should've said something. I should've done something. I was the one who pissed him off.* She sighed heavily, barely acknowledging the traffic that flew past her.

The sidewalks were packed with people, everyone out enjoying the nice weather. The promise of summer was hovering, darkening the sky to a deep piercing blue and gentling the wind to a warm breeze. Val couldn't wait for summer. Summer meant no school and no school meant no Kenny and all the crap that went along with him.

She'd searched for Allison after lunch but couldn't find her. She even checked with the nurse's office but she wasn't there either. When the last bell of the day rang, she never came to her locker. Val wondered if she cut.

Probably did.

She raked a hand through her hair, pulling hard at her ponytail. *Idiot, idiot, idiot, you should've said something. She was trying to help you!*

"Valerie?"

She jolted when a hand touched her shoulder. She turned to see her mother standing before her. For a moment, Val blinked stupidly at her then saw that she'd been passing the bakery where her mother worked. She pushed her sunglasses up onto her head.

"Hey, Mom."

Her mother smiled down at her, wiping her hands on a white towel. There was a smudge of flour across one cheek and her hairline seemed lightly dusted with sugar. Val felt the weight inside her chest give a little. Her mother was a hard worker, diligent and as far as Val knew, wasn't afraid of anything. Val wished she had her mother's fearlessness, especially after what had happened at lunchtime today.

"Valerie, hon. You okay?"

"Yeah, I'm okay," Val forced out, feeling her insides shiver with the urge to tell her mother everything.

"Uh oh. I know that look. Come on inside."

Val looked up at her, wondering if something had shown on her face or if her mother was simply psychic.

"No, no, I'm okay. Really, I've got homework and—"

"Come on. In you go," her mother insisted, ushering her inside the bakery.

Val put up little resistance and as the door closed behind them. Her shoulders sagged as if she'd just been given a reprieve from the gallows. She breathed in the smell of baking bread and fresh coffee, the air so thick with flour and pastries she thought that just by standing in one spot, she'd somehow be covered with baked goods.

A huge glass case ran the length of the shop, filled to capacity with bread, rolls, éclairs, cannoli, fritters, danishes, cream puffs, doughnuts, muffins, bearclaws, cookies, cakes, cupcakes and pies. In big clear jars on top of the case were different types of tea bags and coffees, biscotti, and candies. Unless you knew exactly what you wanted when you first walked in, you could be standing at the case for *hours* trying to decide what to buy. And what made everything even more delicious was the fact that Val's mom made most of the stuff, and Val knew from her own personal experience that Mom was a genius in the kitchen.

Small round tables were set up in front of the big front window that faced the busy street. In one corner was a small wood-burning stove that was more for show than anything else. Why smell wood burning when there were cookies and cakes to smell? It was cozy and warm, coaxing many even on the hottest days of the summer to come in and nibble on a scone straight from the oven.

Mom disappeared behind the counter, shouting to her coworker, Marie, that she was taking a break. She came back out and handed Val a plate containing a large chocolate chip muffin, Val's favorite.

"On the house," her mother winked. "And a peace offering, too."

Val took the plate with a smile. "Peace offering for what?"

"For biting your head off this morning."

They sat down at a table near the wall. Normally they'd sit at the window but Val didn't feel like being seen. Her mother sipped at a cup of coffee while Val had a cold glass of milk.

"It's no big deal," she said. "You've been working your butt off. How much sleep have you gotten within the last two days?"

Her mother's eyes, so much like Sam's but without the bitchiness, sparkled over the rim of her cup. "I got a few hours, *Mom*."

Val smirked as she cut the muffin in half. Thin wisps of steam rose up from it. The chocolate chips gleamed wetly, half-melted. Val took a hearty bite before offering her mother the other half. Mom waved it away.

"You should be getting more than a few hours," Val commented, licking chocolate from her fingertips. "God, this is good."

"Then I won't be so cranky?"

"Exactly."

Her mom laughed. "I'll see what I can do."

"Seriously though. You shouldn't be working this much. It's not healthy."

"Neither is that muffin."

"*Mom*."

Her mom sighed. "Valerie, I know. Believe me, you don't have to tell me that. But until your father can land a job somewhere, the money I'm making here is all that we have."

Val propped her chin in her hand. "I could get a job and—"

"No."

"Why not?"

"Because then Sam's going to want one and I don't want her out any more than she usually is."

"So I can't get a job because she's a moron?"

"You can't get a job because your father and I want you to concentrate on your school work."

"But it could help—"

"I *know* it would help," Mom emphasized as she put down her coffee cup. "But seriously, Valerie, with your workload, do you really think you'd be able to handle a job and *not* get burnt out?"

Val looked down at her pastry. "Well, you're getting burnt out."

Mom smiled softly. "Not yet, Valerie. Not yet. But things will get better. You'll see." She touched her fingertips to the back of Val's hand, making her look up. "Now, are you going to tell me what's wrong? You seem a little lost."

Val licked her dry lips and took a deep breath. Then she unloaded, telling her mother everything that had happened at lunch, except for the part about John. *No one* in her family needed to know about that.

"And I just feel so bad," she finished. "I mean, I'm the one who provoked him and God, Allison was just having my back and..." her voice trailed off.

Mom offered a small smile. "Allison's a good friend. Of course, she's going to have your back."

"I know," Val replied, biting her lip, feeling her eyes beginning to burn again. "And she didn't deserve any of what Kenny said."

"Did you try to find her after school?"

"I couldn't find her anywhere."

"Why don't you call her tonight?"

"What if she doesn't pick up?"

"She will."

"But how do you know?"

"Because she's your friend. She was defending you, something that she's done many, many times before. Kenny just happened to know her weak spot, that's all."

"Yeah, him and the whole school now."

"The whole school can go jump off a bridge. Everyone has a weak spot, Valerie and by the time you graduate, everyone's going to have theirs broadcasted at least once."

Val sighed. "I hate high school."

"Yeah, but you're doing so well. Too bad your sister doesn't have your work ethic."

Val snorted.

They chatted for a while longer until her mother had to go back to work. She sent Val off with a quick kiss on the cheek and a bag of muffins.

"Save the cornbread muffin for your father. It's his favorite." Mom waved from the door.

Val's step was lighter as she walked home. *That's what I'll do. I'll call Allison tonight and I'll—*

"Hey, hey, there she is!"

The shout from up ahead brought Val to a sharp halt. Her heart sank to the pit of her stomach when she saw Sam and Audrey hanging out on the stoop in front of her family's apartment building. Okay, this was *not* something she needed right now even with a bag full of freshly-baked muffins in her hand. She turned to look over her shoulder as Audrey waved at her, thinking, *hoping* that maybe there was someone behind her that she was waving to.

Nope. No such luck. Crap.

She slunk towards them, not even bothering to hide the fact that she wasn't happy to see them. They both grinned at her in a way that made Val wonder if she had something hanging out of her nose. Giving them a strange look, Val tried to move around them but Audrey stepped in front of her. Val stared down at her.

"What?"

She glanced over Audrey's shoulder to look at Sam who only quirked an eyebrow at her.

"How'd your day go, Val?" Audrey asked in her nasally voice.

She was like a mini version of Sam except Audrey had brown hair, streaked with blonde highlights. It fell to her shoulders in a straight bob cut, as sleek and shiny as a cat. But she looked like a fox instead. All of her features were even, thin and coming to a point in the center of her face. Her eyes were the color of Hershey's chocolate, quick, assessing and full of the same sarcasm and mockery that plagued Sam's face. Sometimes Val thought that Audrey was more suited to be Sam's sister than she was. Dressed in tight jeans and a light blue shirt that was cut low enough to show off the matching lace bra she wore beneath it, she was a force to be reckoned with, with or without Bryan's permanent addition to her hip.

Who, at the current moment, was nowhere to be seen. Neither was John and for that, Val was eternally grateful.

Val looked from Audrey to Sam then back again. "Uh...fine. How was your day?"

Audrey smiled, flashing even white teeth. "Oh, good, you know? I learned something too and you know me. I hardly ever retain *anything.*"

Val frowned at her.

"So you want to hear what I learned?"

"I guess."

"I learned about you. In a rumor. You want to know how many times *that's* happened?"

Val's face turned bright red. Audrey laughed and the sound was gleeful and cruel at the same time, like a kid pulling wings off of a fly.

"Yeah, none. Which is why I was so *shocked* when I heard about your fight."

Val's eyes went wide. "Fight? What fight?"

"Judging by your appearance, it looks like you handled yourself pretty well," Audrey went on, studying her far too closely. "What do you think, Sam?"

Audrey stepped back out of her way until Sam was in full view of her.

"I'm a little surprised, to say the least," Sam replied with a sarcastic tilt of her pale pink lips.

"There was no fight," Val sputtered. "I mean, when you say fight, I hope you're not referring to, like, a fight-fight with fists flying and—"

"Broken faces and bleeding knuckles?" Sam finished.

"Yeah, because there wasn't anything like that."

Audrey looked disappointed. "You sure?"

"Positive."

"Guess we should've known better," Audrey said to Sam, taking a seat beside her on the steps.

"Guess so," Sam said. "But it would've been nice if it were true."

Val frowned at her. "No, it wouldn't have been nice."

"That's a quick judgment from someone who's never tried it before."

"Getting into a fight isn't exactly high up on my list of things to do."

"You might like it," Audrey said with a shrug.

Val rolled her eyes. She knew Audrey had gotten into a number of fights over the years. Despite being on the small side, she could level most people who were twice her size. Val had the unfortunate opportunity of being present during one such fight. She was pretty sure the girl Audrey had knocked out still had short term memory loss.

"I'd rather keep the bones in my face whole, thank you very much."

Sam snickered. "It might help you if they weren't."

Audrey laughed loudly, giving her a high-five.

Fed up, Val dashed up the concrete stairs, knocking hard against Sam's shoulder with her leg.

"Oh, *that* was mature," Sam sneered after her. "Hey, so are you going to tell me what the fight was about?"

"There was no fight," Val shot back over her shoulder.

"Come on, Val. Just tell me. I'm going to find out anyway."

"Yeah, because your sources are so accurate."

"Val—"

Val slammed the door on her and took the steps two at a time to their apartment. God, she couldn't *stand* her. *Who in the world made her so high and mighty? And Audrey, Sam's little mini-me puppet. Ugh, they're both so stupid, so immature, so...repugnant.*

She let herself into the apartment, dropping her book bag on the floor. Still scowling, she went into the kitchen and threw the bag of muffins on the counter. Only her sister had the power to get her this annoyed and it wasn't fair. She couldn't strum up an ounce of anger when she was facing off with Kenny but with Sam and her idiotic friends, the anger just came roaring to the surface like it had been laying in wait, just searching for the right moment to strike.

"Idiots," she mumbled to herself as she yanked open the refrigerator door.

"Who's an idiot?"

She spun around to see her father leaning against the counter, sipping a cup of coffee. He smiled at her.

"Hey, Dad."

"How're you doing?"

"All right."

"Doesn't sound like it."

"You ever get the feeling that you're surrounded by idiots?"

"Not a day goes by when I don't think about that."

Val nodded before dragging out a can of soda. She turned to face him. "Is there a cure?"

"For idiocy? Not in our lifetime."

"Too bad."

Her dad chuckled. He was dressed in jeans and a flannel shirt with the sleeves rolled up. He looked like he'd just gotten home from work except he wasn't working. Val could see the strain of that clearly in the depths of his dark brown eyes, in the lines of his rough-hewn face. Looking at the gray hairs that had sprouted at his temples seemingly overnight, Val felt like her problems with her sister were so trivial, so unimportant. She kept trying to tell herself that, in the hopes that maybe Sam would cease to bother her, like maybe for the rest of her life but in the heat of the moment, Val's emotions had no restraint whatsoever. So when she was done dealing with Sam's stupidity, she was left feeling like a chump because she knew her parents' problems rivaled hers by like a million times. She sighed, leaning against the fridge as she popped the tab on her soda can.

"Everything okay?" Dad asked quietly.

Val shrugged. "Yeah, I guess—"

"Val almost got in a fight at school today."

Sam breezed into the kitchen, giving Val a hard nudge out of the way as she opened the fridge.

"Sam!" Val exclaimed angrily.

"A fight?" her father said, shocked. "What? What is this? A fight? Val, you?"

"No!" Val said, shooting Sam a dirty look.

"That's not what's going around school."

Sam took out a pitcher of juice and poured herself a glass. She smirked at Val as she took a sip. Val felt her fingers dent the sides of her soda can.

"I don't *care* what's going around school," she snapped. "That doesn't make it true."

"Well obviously there was something," Sam said, turning to their father. "You know how rumors always start with some kind of truth to them."

Dad fixed Val with a stern look. "Val, so help me, you better not be acting stupid the way Sam is. It's bad enough I have to ground her. I don't want to have to ground you, too."

Sam rolled her eyes.

"I was not fighting," Val repeated.

"Well, something happened," he said. "So what was it?"

"Nothing."

"Then why did your sister say that?"

"Because she's a moron."

"Hey!" Sam said affronted.

"Well, you are!"

"Hold it, hold it," he interrupted, stepping between them. "Val, tell me what happened."

Val stared up at him then looked at Sam who leaned against the counter, trying not to laugh. Val shook her head, her ears humming under the force of her anger, the absolute bottomless frustration of dealing with such a—

"Val?" he said, waiting.

Val met his eyes, blinking hard. She let out a sharp breath. "Okay, God. Look, Kenny and I had a disagreement in the cafeteria. That's all."

"Well that doesn't sound fun," Sam muttered into her juice.

"No, it doesn't, does it?" Val snapped at her.

"Disagreement about what?" he asked.

"Dad—"

"A disagreement about what?" he repeated, his voice hardening into a tone that booked no argument.

Val sighed noisily. "He was being his usual annoying self. I said something about his newspaper articles being trash and...he didn't take it well."

Her father continued to stare hard at her, as if willing her to tell him anything else. Val held up her hands.

"That's it. That's all it was, I swear."

Seeming to be satisfied, Dad straightened his shoulders. "That was all?"

"Yes." *Besides the fact that I couldn't even defend my only friend.*

He ran a hand over his mouth, the tension sliding out of his face. "Why would you say his newspaper articles were trash?"

"Because they are."

Her father snorted a chuckle. "Yeah, but that's no excuse to say it out loud."

Sam pushed away from the counter. "Yes, it is, especially when it's true. Kenny's a loser, which is why I'm surprised Val and him don't get along better."

Val scowled at her retreating back as she left the room, taking her glass of juice with her. *I hope you choke on it.*

"He was also the umpire at my softball game the other night," Val said, returning her attention to her father. "He called the game badly on purpose. As much as I hate to agree with anything that Sam says, he *is* a loser and a pain-in-the-ass."

"Kindly refrain from using that kind of language around me. Look, Val, you need to be careful what you say to people. People are crazy. You can't just insult them whenever you feel like it."

"Sam does it."

"Which is why Sam is probably going to get her ass kicked one of these days."

"Nice language," Val chuckled.

He smiled. "Just be careful, all right? If this guy is on the paper with you, that means close proximity and for the sanity of the rest of the newspaper staff, you might want to try and get along with him."

"Yeah, that's not going to happen."

"Well, just ignore him then."

"That's what I try to do. It's like he goes out of his way to sniff me out and annoy me until I go nuts."

"Change your perfume then."

"Dad," she groaned.

"Okay, okay," He laughed, nudging her shoulder. "Now I believe I smell a cornbread muffin in this bag here."

CHAPTER 6

When Allison didn't show up at school for three days in a row, Val finally allowed herself to quietly freak out. She didn't know what else to do. She called Allison, emailed her, even went to her house where her father, blurry eyed and smelling like he hadn't bathed in three days, promptly told her that Allison hadn't been home for days. Then he proceeded to slam the door in Val's face.

Now on the verge of filing a missing person's report, Val got up the nerve to ask someone at the school's front office. Surely if Allison was sick, someone would've called in for her. It turned out Allison's mother had called in sick for her which made Val even more wary because Allison did not have a close relationship with her mother. On more than one occasion Allison had referred to the woman as "the hag."

So maybe Allison had someone call in pretending to be her mother. It wouldn't be the first time she'd done it.

While that seemed more plausible, it didn't help Val figure out where her friend actually was. No one was taking her homework to her either and when Val volunteered, the teachers told her that it wasn't necessary; that Allison would be back in time to make up the work without penalty. Which led Val to believe that they knew more than she did, which in turn, irked her.

Allison was her friend and Val knew less than everyone else did. And there was still the guilt that hung in her stomach like too many over-easy eggs. There was nothing she could do to stop thinking about it either. Every time she was in a newspaper meeting, Kenny was there. He continuously gave her dirty looks and refused to speak to her, making it impossible to get any work done. It was getting to the point where out of sheer frustration Val was tempted to apologize to him. But then she would think of Allison's ash-white face, the way she'd just closed down when Kenny had blasted her about J.R. and the temptation flew right out the window.

Now it was the morning of the fourth day of MIA-Allison. Val sighed heavily as she cleaned her face in the bathroom. She repeatedly told herself that Allison was a big girl. She could handle...whatever it was that she was handling. She didn't need anyone to worry about her. But there was still that tiny sprig of doubt in the back of Val's mind.

It's got to be something more serious than just being sick, Val thought as she went down the hallway to her bedroom. *I mean, three days of school is a lot to miss—*

Her train of thought stopped abruptly as she passed her sister's room. The door was open but there was no sign of her. Curiously, Val peered inside, the shopping bags on the floor by the bed catching her eye. Val frowned then her eyebrows rose when she saw the hot pink iPod on the night table.

Where in the world did she get an iPod?

Before Val could stop herself, she stepped inside the room. She ignored the flash of *danger zone* in the back of her mind as she picked up the small device. Then she looked down into the closest shopping bag and saw something black and leathery.

What...

"Val."

She bit back a scream as she whirled around.

Justin stood in the doorway, giving her a strange but amused look.

"Geez, man," Val said, holding her hand over her heart. "Don't do that."

"What're you doing in here?"

"Nothing."

He raised his eyebrows as if to say, "Oh really?"

She fidgeted, feeling caught. "None of your business. Now go away."

"She's gonna kill you if she finds you in here."

"Not if you don't say anything."

"I won't have to. She's got this scary ability where she *senses* when people have been snooping around her room."

Val rolled her eyes. "I'm not *snooping.*"

"Okay, looking then."

"Now you're making it sound like a museum."

"Look but don't touch." He looked pointedly at the iPod in her hand.

Val fixed him with a look. "Justin—"

"There a party in here that I should know about?" Sam suddenly appeared behind Justin.

Val jumped again. Justin quickly moved to one side, getting out of the line of fire. Val stood in the center of Sam's room, feeling awkward and stupid. Justin shot her a look. *Told you so*, it seemed to say. There was *no way* an eleven-year-old could master that look but Justin had found a way. Val supposed it was better than him sporting a Justin Bieber haircut.

"Hey," Val said stupidly, fidgeting under the hot glare of her sister's eyes.

Sam leaned casually against the doorjamb, seeming relaxed but her blue eyes flashed dangerously, the ice in them even colder than usual, pinning Val to the spot like a butterfly.

"Val," Sam said, the warning in her voice sending a small shiver of awareness down Val's spine. "What're you doing in here?"

Oh my God, you are so busted.

Val struggled for something witty beneath the cold heaviness of her gaze.

"Uh...well, I was actually looking for something...a shirt, maybe, that I could borrow..."

"Really." Sam's eyes flicked to the iPod in her hand. "I'm not sure anything I have would fit you."

Val swallowed, looking down then back up. "Well—"

Sam suddenly held out her hand, gesturing. "Give it to me."

"I—"

"Val, freakin' give it to me. You have no right to be in here."

Val felt her cheeks flush. "Look, I...how do you even have an iPod?"

It wasn't what she'd meant to say but it came out anyway. A tremor went through Sam's body like she was physically trying to keep from launching herself at Val. Val kind of didn't blame her. She'd be super pissed off too if she discovered Sam in her bedroom. But still, an iPod and all these clothes—

"You have three seconds to get your ass out of my room," Sam warned, her voice low and careful.

"I—"

Sam darted forward, snatching the iPod from Val's hand. Her nails scratched the center of Val's palm and she winced. Sam shoved her finger into Val's face.

"Get out of here. Now."

Val bit her lip. "Sam, what're you doing with this stuff—ow!"

She cried out as Sam grabbed her arm, fingers biting into her bicep and started dragging her towards the door.

"Ow! Sam, let go! Let go—"

"You stay the hell out of here!" she snapped angrily, her pale face flushed and tight.

"Let go!"

"What in the world is going on in here?" her father boomed, appearing in the doorway.

Justin stood to one side of him, looking worried and anxious. Val found herself not caring whether Justin had brought their father into this or not. She could feel her bones creaking under the strength of Sam's grip.

"She won't let go—"

Sam shoved her arm away. "She was in my room without asking, snooping around—"

"She has an iPod, Dad and all these new clothes," Val cut her off in an attempt to save herself.

She rubbed at her arm as she returned Sam's glare. God, she'll probably have finger-shaped bruises.

"What?" Her father frowned, eyes darting back and forth between Sam and Val. "How do you—"

"Ugh, my God," Sam said disgustedly. "It's all Audrey's, okay? God, it's not that big of a deal. Maybe if you had just asked—" she spat at Val.

"Like that would've stopped you from going psycho at me? What is your problem, grabbing me like that? That hurt!"

"My problem is you! You have no right to be in here!"

Dad thundered over them "Why do you have Audrey's stuff?"

Sam threw her hands up. "She's letting me borrow the iPod, and she was cleaning out her closet and asked me if I wanted to look at any of her clothes before she tossed them." She glared at her sister. "Is that okay with you? You satisfied now?"

Val stared at her, frowning.

He sighed. "Val, you know better. Seriously, you'd have a fit if Sam did this to you."

Sam crossed her arms over her chest, raising her chin.

"Now, come on," he went on. "You guys are going to be late for school."

"Wait, wait, wait," Sam said. "That's it? You're not going to ground her or anything?"

"Oh, come *on*," Val moaned.

"I'm serious. She invaded my privacy!"

"It's not like I went digging. Everything was out in plain sight and your door was open!"

"That's not an invitation for you to come on in and touch everything."

"Hey!" he shouted. "Enough. School. Now." He walked away, muttering under his breath.

Sam gave a rude snort then shoved Val out of her room. "You stay *out*, got it? Do I need to put a sign up?"

She slammed the door so hard, the walls shook.

Val stared hard at the closed door, angry and unsettled, like she was missing something. She glanced down at Justin, who'd remained quiet through the whole thing. His dark eyes were troubled. Val's frown deepened. What Sam had said about everything belonging to Audrey—there'd been a faint flickering in her eyes. It was so slight, so quick, had it been on anyone else's face, Val would've missed it. But she hadn't missed it. Because Sam was her sister. Sam was family, like it or not and they all knew each other's quirks and idiosyncrasies. And that faint flickering in Sam's eyes?

It meant she was lying.

CHAPTER 7

She thought about it the whole way to school. What was Sam hiding? This of course was followed immediately by, *why do you care?*

Why indeed?

Sam's business was Sam's business and she always made an effort to keep it that way—which was fine. But it didn't seem fair that while their parents were struggling with money, Sam was toting around an iPod and brand new clothes. Val didn't buy for a second that any of it was Audrey's. So then if it wasn't Audrey's, where did Sam get the money for all that stuff? She didn't have a job and she wasn't dating anybody who would buy those things for her.

It was weird and Val wondered if she should bother wasting the brain power on it. She knew that even if she asked Sam flat out, her sister would simply sneer at her and tell her to mind her own business. It would be like trying to get blood from a stone. The thought of coaxing Sam into something that even remotely resembled a conversation was enough to turn Val away from it all together and by the time she arrived at school, she'd made the decision not to worry about it. Sam prided herself on being clever and anyone who thought otherwise was reviled.

Let her worry about it, Val thought to herself as she made her way to homeroom.

The door to the girls' bathroom swung open and Val stopped short when Allison came out.

"Allison?"

The sight of her friend was such a blowback that for a moment Val thought she was hallucinating. But then Allison was smiling at her and the relief that went through her was staggering.

"Hey Val."

"Oh my God, hey!" Val choked out. "Are you all right? What happened? I tried calling you but no one picked up and then I went to your house and your dad was—"

"Val—Val, whoa, hey, slow down," Allison chuckled, holding up her hand. "Take a breath. I'm okay, really."

Val reached out to touch her arm, struggling to stem her babbling. "I tried to get your homework for you, you know so you wouldn't be behind but your teachers—whoa!"

She darted forward, grabbing at Allison's arm as her friend swayed dangerously on her feet.

"Allison, what—"

"Oh, God," Allison moaned and it was only then that Val realize how horrible she looked. Her skin was pasty and shiny with sweat. The heavy purple bags under her eyes stood out like half moons. The T-shirt and sweatpants she wore looked like they'd been slept in and her hair was limp and unwashed. But what was worse than her appearance was the look in her eyes. It was dull and teeming with anguish and something like pain. Panic began to sink its talons into Val's brain and she hovered closer as Allison sagged against the wall. Her hands were low on her stomach like she was having bad cramps and Val thought for a second maybe that's what it was but cramps were never *this* bad, where she looked ready to collapse.

Val chewed on her lip. "Allison, what's wrong?" she asked, trying to keep the alarm out of her voice. "What happened to you? Do you want to go see the nurse? What—"

"I'm okay," she murmured, closing her eyes.

Val shook her head in disbelief. "No, you're not. Dude—"

"Val, I'm fine," Allison repeated, looking at her.

Her eyes were cloudy and wet like she was trying not to cry. Val stared back at her, torn between dragging her to the nurse's office and hugging her. She clenched her fingers into the hem of her shirt to keep from doing neither.

"Allison—

"Come on. We're going to be late for homeroom."

She pushed away from the wall and started walking, well actually, she started shuffling, very slowly down the hallway. Her steps dragged and her shoulders hunched like she was in pain. Val bit her tongue, wanting again to urge her to see the nurse or go home or *something*. Anything was better than watching her painful shambling down the hallway.

They made it to homeroom. Trying to hover discreetly now, Val waited next to her as she handed their homeroom teacher a doctor's note then went to sit down. Allison eased into her seat slowly like someone who'd just thrown their back out. Val took her seat behind her, watching worriedly as Allison put her head down on her desk. God, she had so many questions, so many things to say, starting with "I'm sorry." But Allison didn't seem interested in talking or anything else for that matter. Val sighed softly, her knee bouncing with impatience.

Because of Allison's doctor's note, she was allowed to leave ten minutes before every bell. She was also allowed access to the elevators. That alone sent another slice of panic through Val. Whatever had happened to Allison, it was obviously serious enough for her to have to stay away from the stairs. Honestly, Val couldn't even imagine how long it would take her friend to make it up one flight. But she was happy to know that Allison had nominated her to carry her book bag.

As they walked along the quiet empty hallway, Val kept sneaking glances at her. Allison seemed oblivious to her presence. There was a crease between her eyebrows as if she were lost inside her own head. Val tried not to take it personally. They waited for the elevator in silence. Val shifted uncomfortably. It was odd. She'd never felt awkward or weird around Allison until now. The whole not-knowing thing was worse than the not-talking. Suddenly Allison bent over, gasping. Val dropped Allison's book bag and grabbed her shoulder.

"Allison!"

Allison's shoulder heaved beneath her hand and she tried weakly to pull away but Val held on. She pushed Allison's hair back, trying to see her face.

"Allison? Oh my God, what's wrong? Talk to me."

The sounds that came from Allison's mouth were horrible. Tiny, wheezing gasps that sounded like her very being was being pulled out by the roots. Val curled her arm around Allison's shoulders, looking around frantically.

"Allison!" The elevator doors slid open. "Here, come on, get inside," Val said desperately, guiding her into the elevator.

Allison scuffled inside. Val propped her up against the wall, moving her gently. She smoothed Allison's hair back from her face, her own hands shaking.

"Oh my God," she said, her voice strangled with indecision. "Allison, you need to see the nurse—"

Allison suddenly gripped her wrist. Val jumped, the contact snapping her eyes to meet Allison's. Her eyes were bright and they bored into Val's like laser beams.

"No. No nurse."

"Why not?" Val exclaimed, feeling very close to freaking out.

"Because she can't do anything about it, that's why," Allison gasped out, blinking hard at the ceiling. "It's already taken care of."

Val shook her head, confused. "What—"She cut herself off and stabbed at the button to close the doors. As they slid closed, she turned back to Allison, her jaw set. "Look, you better start talking. I am ready to freak the hell out on you and I really don't want to because you seem to be in a lot of pain. So please, *please* tell me what's going on."

She stared imploringly into Allison's face, willing her to speak. But Allison continued to stare upwards, her throat convulsing as she swallowed hard. Val waited—*made* herself wait.

The elevator doors sprang open. Val jumped and whirled around. Two people stood there, a guy on crutches and a girl who held his books. Val flashed a quick smile.

"Sorry, guys. This one's taken." She hit the button to close the doors again.

"Hey—!" the girl cried, offended.

Val faced Allison once more and was surprised to see her looking at her with a small smile on her face.

"Nice," she murmured.

Val shook her head. "Don't change the subject."

Allison sighed and dropped her gaze to the floor. Her chest shuddered as she sucked in a few deep breaths. Val watched her carefully. Slowly, Allison raised her head again. Val felt like she'd been sucker punched when she saw her eyes glassy with unshed tears. Concern tightened her stomach into impossible knots and she went to Allison's side, immediately curling an arm around her shoulders once more. Allison sagged into her a little.

"I...I..." she swallowed and the sound was almost audible.

Val waited as she tried again.

"I got rid of it."

"What?" Val said, looking at her, uncomprehending.

The look that Allison gave her was so sad, so forlorn that Val found that she had to suppress tears of her own.

"It's gone."

"What? What's gone?"

Allison let out a sound that was a lot like a sob. "The baby, Val. I had an abortion."

Val's jaw dropped and she almost said "what" again out of pure reflex because she was *sure* that she'd heard wrong. Allison's head fell to her shoulder as if in exhaustion and the sudden weight of it made Val curl her arm tighter around her. Val's mouth moved soundlessly.

"Oh...Oh my...oh, Allison, I...I..."

"I found out that day, when Kenny was being an asshole in the cafeteria," Allison said softly, her voice tired and strained. "What a day that turned out to be."

Val bit her lip and looked down at her, at the gamut of emotions that flew across Allison's face—disgust, shame, disappointment, guilt, fear and above all, a deep-rooted sadness.

"Oh, man. Allison, I...I'm so sorry," she fumbled.

"For what?"

Val scrambled for something profound to say, something that would ease the pain of this moment and take the heaviness of it away because even though it hadn't happened to her, Val felt like her brain was being crushed beneath the weight of it, like someone had thrown an extra twenty tons of books into her book bag. She didn't even want to think about how heavy the weight was for Allison.

"I...I don't know," Val said stupidly. "I—"

"It was J.R.'s."

Val jolted hard enough so that Allison picked her head up to look at her then sighed. "Yeah."

Trying to think, Val shook her head to clear it. "Wait, wait, I thought...I thought you were on the pill. I mean—"

"Yeah, well, like *an idiot*, I never got around to refilling my prescription and..." Her voice trailed off.

"But didn't you tell him? Didn't you tell him that—"

"Yeah, I told him."

Val felt her back seize up. "He didn't force you, did he?"

Allison's cheeks suddenly flushed and it was almost a relief to see color on her face. "I was high. I didn't know what end was up, and he wasn't about to pass up an opportunity to get laid, pill or no pill."

"Did you tell him that you were pregnant?"

Allison gave her a look. "Come on, Val. You really think he'd believe me?"

Val felt a flare of anger. "I don't see why he wouldn't. You've been nothing but loyal to him from the start."

Allison gently pulled away from her, teeth worrying her bottom lip as she looked down at the floor.

"You didn't go by yourself, did you? I mean, I would've gone if—"

"No, no, my mom went with me."

Val felt a sting of envy. As if sensing it, Allison touched her arm.

"I couldn't tell you, Val. I couldn't...I couldn't tell anyone. I just couldn't. I didn't want you to think that I was...I don't know, I just..." She sighed harshly as if aggravated with herself that she couldn't get the words to come out.

Val nodded, trying to understand as much as she could.

"All I knew was that I couldn't keep it," Allison went on. "I'm sixteen. I know I'm not ready for anything big like having a kid. I mean, honestly, could you even see me trying to change a diaper?"

Val gave a small smile. "Not really."

Allison's mouth trembled like she was trying to smile too but failed. A single tear rolled down her cheek. "I feel so horrible, Val. I feel...so gross and guilty and stupid. I just...I don't know, I don't feel like me anymore."

A soft sob escaped her and Val immediately, instinctively wrapped her up in a hug. Allison cried into her shoulder. Val held her close, feeling her heart pound painfully at the sound of her sobs.

God, this was...there are no words for this.

And there weren't. She held her friend as she cried. She rubbed her hand up and down Allison's back, the way Val's mother used to do when Val was sick as a child.

The elevator doors slid open again. Val grunted in annoyance then froze when she saw Kenny standing there.

Oh fabulous.

Allison pulled away, wiping at her tear-streaked face. She rolled her eyes as Kenny cocked a leg and gave them a smug smile.

"I always knew there was something between you two."

Val gave him a dirty look, suddenly fiercely protective of her friend. She even moved in front of her a little, as if to shield her.

"Are you serious, dude? Can you not see that she's upset?"

"Aw, are you guys having a lovers' spat?"

"You are so ridiculous," Allison said, shaking her head and stabbing at the elevator button to get to the third floor.

"Just doing my job," he said as he jumped into the elevator just as the doors slid closed.

Val groaned. "Dude, come on—"

"So what's the scoop?" he asked, his eyes bouncing from Allison to Val then back again. "We all know Val is mentally retarded and needs to take the elevator but Allison? What's your excuse?"

"Oh, that's nice. So now you're talking to me only to insult me?"

"I'm not about to let the fact that you're blind to talent stop me from doing my job."

"Right. Blind to talent, that's me."

"It is. Now onto more important news. What's going on in this elevator even as we speak? Allison?"

"None of your business," Allison sighed, rubbing at her forehead.

"Val—"

"None of your business."

"How about off the record?"

"Do you even know what that means?"

"Absolutely. I just can't guarantee that it *stays* off the record, that's all."

"That's generally the whole point of off the record."

Kenny grinned. "Not on my watch."

Val rolled her eyes. The elevator couldn't move fast enough.

"Man, you guys are no fun."

Neither girl answered him and when the elevator doors opened on their floor, Kenny bounced out ahead of them. "Let me know when you change your mind."

"You'll be first to know," Allison mumbled.

"God, I can't stand him," Val said as he walked away.

"I don't think anybody can."

The bell rang and the hallway was suddenly filled with students. Allison winced and shuffled to one side as the tide of people flowed past them.

"You want to come by the bakery after school today?" Val asked. "Get something to eat? Some tea maybe? I know how much you like the earl gray they have there."

For a second, Allison looked like she was going to say no. But then she nodded.

"You know, that actually sounds really good."

CHAPTER 8

Halfway through the day however, Allison told Val she wanted to go home early. The school nurse took one look at her and granted her permission which was very surprising because normally a student would have to be in death's throes or bleeding from the head before she allowed anyone to leave school property. Allison gave her a sad smile before Val left her in the nurse's capable hands and that smile stayed with Val throughout the remainder of the day.

She walked home alone, her thoughts making her deaf to the world around her. She couldn't for a moment understand or even comprehend what her friend was going through and it both frustrated and relieved her. This was heavy and she wanted to help Allison in any way she could but she just didn't know *how*. And while Val tried not to be cranky about Allison not trusting her enough to at least go with her to...wherever she had to go to take care of this, Val was also somewhat grateful. She was pretty certain she would've gone had she been asked, but sitting in a waiting room with other would-be mothers who had all made colossal mistakes, who would all soon be non-would-be mothers—well, Val wasn't *that* sure of herself. While she was confident that she would've definitely remained at Allison's side no matter what, there was another darker part of her that would've wanted to head straight for the exit.

Following that train of thought, Val began to wonder. Allison was stupid for J.R. That was a scientifically proven fact. They also had sex—a lot of sex, according to Allison. So why didn't she just get her birth control prescription refilled? Why wait? Why take the chance that something like this could happen?

Val wasn't sure if there was a logical explanation but she was hardly one to say anything. She was sadly aware of how far behind she was. All of sixteen and she hadn't even had a decent kiss yet. *And that smooch with Dave by the bleachers at the softball field when I was fourteen totally does not count*, she told herself emphatically.

She shuddered at the memory. He had wanted to go further after hanging out only twice but in those two times, Val found herself enjoying his company less and less. He'd been pushy and a little rough, and they weren't even a couple when he suggested that they have sex in his parents' basement. Not that being a couple mattered to most guys, she knew, but she didn't need or want the outcome of that little get-together going around school either. She knew that if Dave thought she was like that, it wouldn't take very long for others guys to get the same idea.

There were a lot of girls who did what she wouldn't, and sometimes Val wondered if perhaps they were onto something. That maybe by having sex without being in a relationship, it was an easier thing to handle because really, most people at school who had a boyfriend or a girlfriend, well, they were just flat out miserable. Always arguing, fighting, complaining, breaking up, getting back together, breaking up, hooking up with somebody else, then getting back together. It all went around and around in one big endless loop. So it was either have sex with anyone, be considered a slut, and end up in a situation like Allison, or be in a relationship and be miserable and *still* end up in a situation like Allison.

Val's head began to ache.

Suddenly there was an eye-watering blare of bass from a car radio coming down the street. Wincing, she looked over her shoulder to see Mark Colitto's tricked out black Ford Explorer shoot past her to park in front of her apartment building. The chrome rims sparkled, the paint was like a mirror and when Sam got out of the front passenger seat, Val did a double take.

I thought they broke up.

Sam shoved something in her back pocket and slammed the car door without a word. Val wasn't close enough to see her face but she could tell by the way she walked that she wasn't happy.

"Thanks, babe!" Mark called out from behind the wheel.

Ignoring him, Sam marched up the steps and disappeared inside the building. Mark sped away, laughing, nearly side-swiping a delivery truck as he peeled off down the street. Val frowned. Sam was another one—dating guys who were complete and utter scumbags. It was clearly an epidemic and Val could only hope that someday someone would be able to explain the attraction because she couldn't see it at all.

She followed her sister inside. As she stepped into the apartment and closed the door behind her, she could hear bottles and cartons rattling in the fridge. It was angry rattling, too, and Val made the smart decision to bypass the kitchen all together. Of course, she snuck a peek inside as she went past then abruptly wished that she hadn't. She came to a stop, blinked then blinked again.

There was a fifty dollar bill sticking out of the back pocket of Sam's jeans.

As if sensing she was being watched, Sam turned away from the fridge and pinned her sister with a look.

Caught again.

At least she wasn't in Sam's room this time.

"What're you staring at?" Sam snapped at her, popping the tab on a can of soda.

The automatic retort of "nothing" died on Val's lips as she took in Sam's somewhat haggard appearance. Her hair was mussed up as if it'd been grabbed and tugged on, her lips were red and swollen and there was a stain on the front of her shirt. Honestly, it was the worst Val had ever seen her since two years ago when Sam had fallen asleep on the beach and Val had forgotten to wake her up. The shade of red Sam had turned was pretty funny but then the blisters and sun poisoning set in and it suddenly lost its humor.

Val met her eyes then asked hesitantly, "You okay?"

Sam raised an eyebrow and cocked a hip. It was frighteningly synchronized. "Yeah. Why wouldn't I be?"

Her tone matched the look in her eyes—tense, angry and skittish, like an animal being forced into a corner. Truth be told, it made Val more than a bit curious to see her sister so unruffled. She watched as Sam took a swig of soda and swished it around in her mouth like mouthwash before swallowing it.

"What?" Sam bit off and it sounded like a firecracker.

"Nothing, nothing,"

"Then why're you still standing there?"

"I live here too. I can stand where I want."

"God, Val, when are you going to grow up?"

Val gave her a doubtful look. She'd always considered herself the more mature one even if Sam was older than her. "When are you going to stop seeing losers like Mark?"

Sam blanched, which was kind of neat since she was so pale already. She recovered quickly though, her usual cool indifferent mask sliding in place to hide the...panic? Shame? Unwillingly, Val found herself becoming more and more intrigued. It was like watching a really bad movie but instead of turning it off, you still watched it because you wanted to see how it ended.

"I am not seeing Mark," Sam said coldly. "Not that it's any of your business."

"I just saw you with him."

Sam's fingers went white around her soda can. "What? Where?"

"Just now. Dropping you off. I thought you guys broke up or something."

"We were never dating," Sam scoffed. "He's a freaking loser."

"Then why—"

"I just got a ride from him, okay, Val? God. You gonna run and tell Mom and Dad on me, like you always do?"

Val moved her head back. "I've never told on you—"

"Yeah, right."

"I haven't! Whenever you get in trouble, it's because of you, not me."

"How am I supposed to believe that now that I know you're spying on me?"

Val's eyes widened in disbelief. *See what happens when you're curious? It comes back to bite you in the ass.* "I'm not spying on you! Are you nuts?" she exclaimed.

"You said—"

"I was walking home and Mark flew past me in that ridiculous clown-car of his. I saw you get out, okay? Does that sound like spying to you?"

Sam was grinding her teeth together so hard, Val was sure her molars were dissolving into dust. The tension crackled between them and Val, as usual, was unsure of where it came from. They were sisters. Weren't sisters supposed to get along? Weren't they supposed to keep each other's secrets and watch out for one another? Were they supposed to snap and attack one another like two cats fighting over a piece of furniture? Looking at her sister's tightly coiled body and flashing blue eyes, she thought with a resigned sigh that *yup, we are supposed to be this mean to each other.*

"I don't know why you're so concerned with the people I surround myself with," Sam retorted. "The people you hang out with aren't much better."

It was Val's turn to scoff. "Oh really? Name one."

"Allison."

Val froze.

Sam grinned and it was unpleasant and mean. "Oh yes. I heard about her. In fact, the whole school did. Getting knocked up by J.R. of all people. And you're running your mouth about Mark?"

Val's mouth went dry. "I...It...It was a mistake. That's all—"

"Yeah?" Sam laughed. "What happened? She and J.R. trip and fall down on top of each other, naked and oops?"

Val glared at her. "You know, you don't like it when I talk about your friends so why don't you keep your mouth shut about mine?"

"Exactly. You don't like it anymore than I do. So why don't you at least try to mind your own business and I'll try to stay out of yours?"

"You know, I was just asking you if you were okay."

Sam rolled her eyes. "Oh, you're worried about me? How cute."

"I'm serious. You look like crap. You've got some kind of stain on your shirt and your hair's messed up."

Sam took two strides and leaned down into her face. "Thanks so much for pointing that out," she said harshly, her voice low and angry. "I didn't know my appearance was so important to you."

"Sam—"

Sam walked out of the kitchen, knocking Val's shoulder hard as she passed. Sputtering, Val caught herself against the counter. She heard the breathless *whish* as Sam slammed her bedroom door shut.

Val stayed where she was, rubbing her shoulder. Her jaw ached and she realized that she'd had her teeth clenched so tightly, she probably had a mouthful of tooth dust too. Slowly she unclenched her jaw. It took her longer than usual to calm down and when she did, she picked up the phone to call Allison.

CHAPTER 9

Val waited for Allison at her locker the next morning. She winced at the sound of too-loud laughter, too-thick conversations about homework and television shows, and too-harsh lockers slamming shut up and down the hallway, echoing and re-echoing inside her head like a hammer on a sheet of metal. She felt cranky and tired, having barely slept the night before, plagued by dreams of a house with too many rooms and not enough exits. When her alarm finally went off, her eyes were puffy and crusted shut and it had taken all of her strength to peel herself out of bed.

Now as she sagged against the lockers, she wondered if she should just call it quits and go home. Plead the old "I-don't-feel-good" excuse. Although she'd probably get kicked out of the nurse's office and sent back to class anyway, so why bother?

It was all Sam's fault. Val had gone out of her way to express concern for her and where did it get her? No sleep and an ache in her body that no amount of *Aleve* could conquer. It wasn't fair and it annoyed her more than usual that while she suffered for what she thought were good intentions, Sam had flounced past her out the door without a word, looking as radiant and put together as usual. It was like yesterday's trampled look had never existed.

Val sighed, squeezing her eyes shut. She always told herself not to bother with Sam and she always went against that logic. She figured by now she would have learned her lesson. She glanced down the hallway in time to see Allison come around the corner. She was walking better than yesterday, still slow but not shuffling. There was more color to her face even if it was still drawn and tired looking but it was good to see her nonetheless. The sight of her extinguished the frustration she'd felt last night when she had tried repeatedly to get a hold of her on the phone, only to be told every time that she was resting.

"Hey, man," Val greeted her with a smile.

Allison flashed a smile that didn't seem particularly friendly. "Hey, stalker. Heard you blew up my phone last night."

Val looked sheepish. "Sorry. Just wanted to see how you were doing."

"How do you think I'm doing, Val? Seriously. You think I'm having fun or something?"

She shook her head and moved around Val to open her locker. Val blinked at her.

"Uh...no, I know you're not having fun. I was just—"

"What?" Allison cut in sharply, her tone callous.

Val took a step back. "I was just...I just wanted to see how you were feeling, man, that's all. I'm sorry if—"

"Well, if my mom tells you I'm resting, then I'm resting. There's no need to call me five hundred times."

"I didn't call you five hundred times," Val said with a frown.

Allison got her books out of her locker then slammed it shut. "Whatever."

She walked away from her. Too stunned to move, Val had a moment to think, *what did I do?* before going after her.

"Hey, wait, let me carry your—"

"I got it, Val."

Val touched her shoulder. "You're not supposed to—"

"I said I got it," Allison snapped.

Val felt her cheeks redden as several people around them turned to watch. She bit the inside of her cheek. "Allison, will you wait a minute? What—"

Allison pulled away from her with an annoyed grunt. "God, will you stop? Just stop. It's not always about you, you know."

Val stared at her, confused and speechless. Allison shook her head, started to walk away then turned back.

"I'm going to ask Julia to carry my stuff from now on so you won't have to, okay?" She headed off down the hallway without waiting for a reply.

Not that Val had one. She could only stand there, blinking stupidly, as the tide of students flowed around her. She had no idea how long she stood there, brain-numb, until the bell announced its presence in all its shrill and ear-piercing glory. Moving in a daze, Val made her way to homeroom. She entered the stairwell, nearly getting knocked over as someone tore past her and up the steps. She reached the landing and felt a hard tug on her arm.

"Hey."

Audrey was suddenly in her face, her mouth set in a hard white line, her eyes like bits of brown stone. Without waiting for an answer, she pulled Val to one side, out of the flow of people that moved up and down the stairs.

"Now what—" Val started to say.

"Was your sister home last night?"

Val stared at her. "What?"

"Was your sister home last night?" Audrey repeated as if she were talking to a handicapped person.

"Uh, yeah..."

"She was."

"Yeah."

"You're sure?"

Val shook her head. This was just too much to be handling in a five minute timespan. "I...yeah, yeah, I'm sure."

Audrey leaned back on her heels, her hands at her hips, giving Val a suspicious look. It didn't take long for Val to fidget beneath the scrutiny.

"What?"

"You don't seem sure."

"Oh, for—Audrey, didn't you call her? You guys talk on the phone every night. You would probably know better than I would if she were home or not."

Audrey raised a perfectly-tweezed eyebrow. "Don't get smart with me."

Val opened her arms. "Well, what do you want me to say? She was at the dinner table and she's supposed to be grounded, as you very well know, so I'm assuming she was home unless she was stupid enough to sneak out. Again." Without waiting for Audrey to respond, Val spun away from her and ran up the stairs.

"Val!" Audrey shouted angrily after her.

Val ignored her, racing up the steps to the third floor. *God, what the hell was going on around here?*

She ducked into homeroom, ignoring everyone and plunked down in her seat. If she was lucky, the day would fly by.

ભ૭ભ૭

Of course, the day absolutely crawled, through molasses and quicksand. Every time she looked up, she saw Allison and Julia walking together, talking and laughing. Every time she looked down, she saw red and felt unexpected tears stab at her eyes. She sat by herself during lunch, trying to ignore the looks and whispers around her because no one at school was dumb enough by half to see that something was obviously wrong if Allison was sitting with Julia and not her.

Julia.

Val scoffed to herself. What a joke. She was a self-proclaimed boyfriend-stealer and a bitch to boot. She made Sam look like a Girl Scout and Val was pretty sure that Julia had been one of the girls whom J.R. had cheated on Allison with. Of course, judging by the way they were suddenly buddy-buddy, that little fact didn't seem to bother Allison that much anymore. Val sank her head further into the history book she had propped in front of her like a shield. Her lunch tasted like wet cardboard.

"Uh oh, trouble in paradise?"

The voice from above her made her cringe. She glanced up with a glare as Kenny took a seat across from her, grinning as if he'd just struck gold. Val tried to hide behind her textbook.

"Go away," she mumbled.

"Oh, come on," he said cheerfully. "Your partner-in-crime has ditched you. There's only one word I want to hear out of your mouth right now, Delton."

She gave him a bored look.

Kenny bobbed his eyebrows up and down. "Revenge."

Val rolled her eyes. "This isn't exactly '*The Count of Monte Cristo*', Kenny."

"The who?"

"Never mind. Could you just go away please?"

"Aw, c'mon, Val," he said, leaning forward. "Everyone's dying to know what happened. You guys are always joined at the hip and now the hip has been severed. C'mon, dude, spill."

"There's nothing to tell."

"Sure there is."

"No, there really isn't. I don't know what happened."

He considered her for a moment. "This doesn't have anything to do with her...personal problem, does it?"

She looked at him. "How did you find out about that?"

"I never reveal my sources."

Val put her book down. "No, I'm serious. My sister said something about it yesterday and now here you are, talking about it. How did it make its way around school so fast?"

Kenny gave her a look. "Dude, are you serious? Like you couldn't tell just by looking at her? Cramps don't make you take the elevator and J.R. isn't exactly subtle when it comes to his choice of chicks to bang."

She winced. "Thanks for that image."

He grinned. "No problem. Hey, did your breakup have something to do with that?"

"It is not a break up."

"Well, it sure seems like it to me. A very strange and distorted breakup but a breakup nonetheless."

"A lot of things seem strange and distorted to you, Kenny. That's because you're you."

"And you are jealous."

"Sorry, dude. I think you're confusing fantasy with reality again."

CHAPTER 10

Val sprawled across the living room floor, surrounded by homework. Justin was across the room from her on the couch, engrossed in a comic book. It was quiet, peaceful, something she needed after the crap of a day she'd had. She could see the phone in the kitchen from where she was on the floor. Her fingers itched to call Allison, to demand that she tell her what exactly she'd done to get the cold shoulder. But she knew Allison wouldn't answer and Val didn't want to embarrass herself any further. Sooner or later, though, they were going to have a talk.

People just didn't end friendships on a whim. It wasn't right and it wasn't fair. She and Allison had been through a lot together and their history didn't justify an instant cutoff like the one Allison had administered earlier that day.

The doorbell rang.

Justin leapt to his feet, comic book flying across the couch.

"See who it is first!" Val called after him.

She heard the scrape of chair legs and then Justin peering through the eyehole in the front door.

"The three amigos," he called back.

Val snickered.

"Not funny," Sam said, coming out of the kitchen. She gave Justin a playful shove as he vaulted past her, back to the couch. Val kept her eyes on her schoolwork but listened intently as Sam threw open the front door. "Hey guys—" she started to greet them.

"Oh, so you're alive," Val heard Bryan snap smartly.

"Uh—"

"Where the hell have you *been?*" Audrey whined.

Val frowned.

"What do you mean? I've been here," Sam said.

"Yeah, obviously. You were supposed to meet us after school today."

There was a sound that was like Sam had slapped a hand to her forehead. "Oh crap."

"Yeah, oh crap," Bryan said dryly.

"Oh, man, sorry guys, I forgot."

"Dude, what has been up with you lately?" Bryan went on. "You forgot today, which makes it twice this week and then you forgot three times last week. What the hell—"

"You keeping a scorecard?" Sam cut in.

Val almost laughed but held herself in check.

Then John's deep voice said, "Come on, girl. What's up? What you been doing?"

He was the only one showing a smidge of concern and for some unknown reason, Val felt her face heat up. She tried in vain to concentrate on her homework but now it was impossible. If Sam was involved in anything that would result in her having fifty bucks in her back pocket, her friends would be the ones to get it out of her. She found herself subconsciously leaning forward, towards the conversation. Her pen was drawing squiggly indecipherable lines on her notebook paper. She glanced over at Justin. He was watching her but there was a glazed-over look on his face that said he was listening too. Val almost smiled. It made her feel a little better that she wasn't the only one eavesdropping.

For the better good, she told herself firmly. *As Sam's younger siblings, we have to look out for her. It has to be like a prerequisite or something. It's in the job description.*

Not that Sam would appreciate it, a small voice added unhelpfully in the back of her mind.

"Nothing, really," Sam was saying now. "I—"

"Oh, come on," Bryan said, annoyed. "You've been avoiding us."

"I have not and will you please keep your damn voice down?"

"What's going on, Sam?" came the quiet rumble of John's voice.

"Nothing, I said. I've just been busy, that's all."

Val gave a small shake of her head. As far as lies went, that was definitely one of Sam's weaker ones.

Apparently Audrey thought so too because she said, "Busy doing what? Homework? I thought Val was the nerd."

Val shot her a dirty look that she couldn't see. Justin hid a smile behind his comic book.

"She is," Sam said, probably with a roll of her eyes. "What, I can't be busy, too?"

"Well, it would've been nice if you'd given us a heads up," Bryan grumbled. "That way we didn't have to wait around with our thumbs up our asses."

"Oh, will you quit whining?" Sam groaned, impatiently. "I'm sorry, all right?"

"Yeah, yeah, "Audrey sighed. "Look, you want to come out for a bit?"

"Can't, dude. You know I'm under house arrest."

"When has that ever stopped you?"

Everyone laughed and the tension in the air dissipated like smoke.

"I'll walk you guys back out," Sam volunteered and that was followed by the door shutting.

Disappointed, Val exchanged a look with Justin. Her brother shrugged.

"What do you think Sam's busy doing?" he asked.

Val shook her head. "I have no idea."

She turned back to her work and Justin went back to his comic book. About ten minutes of relative peace went by before the front door flew open and Sam stormed into the living room. Anger flared out before her like a heat blast from a furnace. She stomped over to Val, her bare feet crinkling her papers.

"Hey!" Val cried. "Get off!"

"What is your problem?" Sam exclaimed angrily.

"Oh geez, now what? Will you get off my homework please?" She tried to pull her notebook out from under Sam's feet. "I'd rather not have your footprints on it when I—"

"Who the hell do you think you are?" Sam cut in, her voice rising. "Who are you to give my friend an attitude?"

Val stopped tugging. "What are you talking about?"

"You think you're some kind of hot shot or something, shooting your mouth off and—"

"Sam, *what* are you talking about?"

"I'm talking about Audrey, moron. She told me you went up to her today with this big freaking attitude and—"

"Oh no! No, no, no!" Val shot to her feet. "No, that is not what happened. Audrey came up to me, all right? *She* came up to *me*."

Sam shook her head. "No—"

"Yes, she did. She came up to me, asking me all these asinine questions—"

"About what?"

"About *you*. What, she didn't tell you that part?"

Sam's mouth snapped shut. She stared down at Val, breathing hard. Val could almost hear the wheels turning in her head. Or maybe it was more like static electricity in there. Who knew?

"What about me?" Sam finally said in a barely-controlled tone.

"She wanted to know if you were home last night."

Sam squinted at her until her eyes were nothing more than slits of blue. "You're such a liar."

"I am *not* lying!"

"Yes, you are," Sam growled, jabbing a finger in Val's face. "Just because your friends don't talk to you anymore doesn't mean you can start talking to mine." She spun away from her, heading towards her room.

Val glared daggers at her back. "Then tell them to stop talking to me!" she hollered after her.

The sound of Sam's bedroom door slamming was her answer. She threw herself back down on the floor, trying unsuccessfully to get the wrinkles out of her homework pages.

"That girl's got a serious attitude problem of her own," she muttered.

"She never used to get that angry before," Justin said quietly. "About anything."

"I know and now it seems like it doesn't take much."

"Do you think it has anything to do with her being 'busy'?"

It should've been hilariously funny to see an eleven-year-old doing air quotes with his fingers but the seriousness of the question stopped her from laughing. Hearing it said out loud made Val's stomach tighten unpleasantly and it was a struggle for her to shake her thoughts away from it.

"I'm going to my room." She packed up her books, fully aware of Justin's eyes burning into her back the whole way down the hallway.

෴෴෴

Later that night, when she'd finally awoken, realizing that once again she'd fallen asleep face first in her textbook, she dragged herself out of bed. The apartment was quiet, filled with shadows and the hush of night. She wiped at her mouth, wincing at the dried drool that snaked along her cheek. She headed for the kitchen to get something to drink.

Gonna have to take a shower in the morning, she thought sleepily.

The sound of whispering, urgent and half-afraid, dragged her to full awareness and she stopped right outside the kitchen. She glanced behind her. Darkness stared back at her and goosebumps popped up along her arms.

"—I *tried.* I don't know what you want me to say."

Val went still, listening, the remains of sleep falling away like silk ribbons being untied from a box.

"—don't you think I know that? I never said—"

Val took a deep breath and carefully, slowly, eased herself closer to the kitchen doorway. She peeked around the corner.

Sam was hunched in a chair at the table, her long white fingers nervously curling the phone cord around and around until it stretched to the point of being pulled out of the wall mount. Her back was to Val but Val could see the muscles of her shoulders shake with every breath she took. Her knee bounced up and down, bumping gently against the underside of the table.

"—no, of course not. I don't—"

Val squinted in the near darkness, straining her ears as Sam's voice dipped and rose faintly.

"No," she suddenly said, louder than she'd meant to.

Val ducked back behind the wall, the chair creaking under Sam's weight. Val bit her lip.

"No," she heard Sam say again, her voice falling to a whisper once more. "No, don't. I said I would do it and I'll do it, okay? Please, just—"

Val felt an unexplainable chill come over her at the sudden fear lacing her sister's tone. She started to look back into the kitchen when she heard footsteps move along the kitchen floor.

She heard the phone being hung up. Panicking, Val danced back a few feet then started forward, praying that Sam wouldn't see how awake she really was. She rubbed at her eye with one hand for good measure and nearly collided with Sam as she left the kitchen. Sam froze at the sight of her.

"Oh, hey," Val said, softly. "Didn't know you were up."

Sam stared at her for a few moments then without a word, walked around her and went back to her room. Val watched her leave, blowing out a long breath when her bedroom door closed. But her relief was short lived.

Who had Sam been talking to? And more importantly, who or what was she afraid of?

CHAPTER 11

The next few days were more of the same. Allison still wasn't talking to her; now she was flat out ignoring Val whenever they were in the same room together. Kenny was his usual annoying, aggravating self, both on the softball field and in school, and the homework assignments seemed endless as teachers tried to cram in as much as they could before the end of the school year.

Inside Val's head however, it was a different story. She had tried desperately ever since she found the clothes and iPod in Sam's room, to keep Sam's business at arm's length. It didn't concern her at all, and Sam would be the first person to tell her so. But there was too much to ignore now.

After the phone call she had overheard, and *the fear* in Sam's voice that kept replaying over and over again in her mind, Val suspected something was definitely going on. Something that Sam had no control over. Something that had her scared.

The Sam that Val knew was fearless, just like their mother. Nothing ever fazed her—not their parents when they caught her sneaking out, not teachers when they caught her cutting class, not any girl or guy who got in her face about something. Nothing, nada, zip. It was the only quality that Val wouldn't have minded sharing with her.

The only problem with this fearlessness was when the moment came and fear finally made itself known—and it always did because everybody was afraid of something—it was way too easy to spot. Like the lone wounded gazelle in a herd that a hungry lion would immediately set its sights on. And if Sam *was* afraid, it wasn't going to take much to bring her down. Fear made people do stupid things, made them act irrationally. Val knew this and she wasn't sure if that was a good thing or a bad thing.

She stood outside her mother's bakery after school, the blustery wind whipping her hair in front of her face. Gray and white clouds roiled together like a big pot of cloudy stew. Every now and then the sun would make an appearance but then it would dodge back into hiding as if it weren't sure it liked what it saw.

Val felt a lot like that, too. She hated being indecisive and that was definitely what she was right now. Talking to her mother about this was iffy, especially since Val had no concrete proof. Sure, she could always mention the clothes and iPod but Sam had that covered pretty easily. Talking to Sam's friends was a big, fat *hell no*. They were as volatile as Sam and if they were showing up at her front door, demanding what Sam was up to then they probably were no closer to finding out anything than Val was.

The door to the bakery suddenly swung open and Allison appeared.

Val froze, standing stock still as her former friend ruffled through the white bag of baked goods she held in the crook of her arm.

Maybe she won't see me.

No such luck.

As if on cue, Allison glanced up and stopped. They stared at each other. The hurt of being rejected so readily had Val looking away from her. She heard the bag rustle then Allison took a breath as if to speak.

Then the bakery door opened again and Julia emerged. "Ugh, they didn't even have blueberry muffins," she complained. "What kind of bakery has no blueberry muffins?"

Allison looked at her then back at Val, her expression unreadable. Julia continued to gripe until she noticed Val and she flashed a sickly sweet smile that left her eyes cold. "Oh, *hey* Val. Tell your mom she needs some blueberry muffins, like now. You ready?" she asked Allison with a flip of her long curly hair.

Val swallowed a mouthful of dust, torn between wanting to scream and wanting to cry or maybe both. She stared hard at the ground as they walked away, not noticing Allison looking back over her shoulder several times as they crossed the street. Biting her lip hard enough to taste blood, she went into the bakery.

For a moment she couldn't see. Then she realized that there were tears in her eyes. Quickly, embarrassed, she wiped them away, gripping the straps of her book bag hard enough to break them.

Her mother appeared behind the counter. "Hey, hon," she called out.

"Hi, Mom," Val said but it came out as a croak. She swallowed hard then tried again. "I hear you're out of blueberry muffins."

Her mother rolled her eyes. "Do you know that girl? She came in with Allison. I thought for sure you would be right behind her—"

"Allison and I aren't really talking anymore."

Mom's eyebrows rose up into her hairline. "Really? How come? How did I miss this?"

Val shrugged. "It's no big deal."

Her mother came around to her side and guided her to a small table. "Of course it is," she frowned, sitting across from her.

Val caught a whiff of bananas coming from her mother's clothes and she smiled a little. "No, it's really not. If she wants to hang out with Julia, then fine. I'm not going to lose sleep over it."

"Looks like you already have," her mother replied gently.

Val sighed. "I don't even know how it happened. She just...stopped talking to me."

"Just like that?"

"Just like that. Said something about it not always being about me, whatever that's supposed to mean."

Her mother frowned. "Well, that doesn't make much sense. You guys have never gotten into any fights or even a disagreement in all the years you've known each other."

Val nodded. "Exactly."

Mom was silent for a moment then said, "You know, she was walking kind of funny. Shuffling like she was afraid to pick up her feet."

Val looked at her, suddenly realizing that her mother didn't know. She pressed her lips together, wondering if she should tell her. Then she figured why not, since their friendship was finished anyway. Leaning forward, she dropped her voice to a whisper. "She had an abortion."

It was almost worth the look of shock on her mother's face. She was speechless for nearly five minutes as she gaped at her daughter.

"What?" she finally breathed.

"It was J.R.'s, the brainless wonder."

Her mother shook her head slowly. "Oh my God. I don't believe it. Wasn't she on the pill?"

"That's the funny part," Val said. "She said she never got around to refilling her prescription."

Mom frowned. "How do you not get around to refilling your prescription? That's ridiculous."

"I know."

"Wow." She shook her head again then narrowed her eyes at Val. "You just better be sure to let me know when you start having sex."

"Mom!" Val exclaimed, her cheeks flushing. She looked around to see if anyone had overheard.

"I'm serious," her mother said firmly. "I don't need to be a grandmother while my daughter's not even legal to vote yet."

Val put her head in her hands. "I cannot believe you just said that."

"And I can't believe your friend is that stupid."

"She's not my friend. Not anymore."

Her mother looked at the wall clock. "I've got to get back to work. You go straight home, okay? No boyfriends."

Val had to laugh. "Sure, because they're just knocking my door down."

Mom stood up and kissed her daughter's forehead. "Give them time, hon. They will."

Val left the bakery in a better mood. Halfway home though she realized she never brought up the Sam issue.

The Sam issue.

Sounds like a magazine. Val sighed as she trudged up the steps of the apartment building. *Tonight. I'll say something to Mom and Dad tonight and—*

"Ow!" she grunted as someone walked into her, knocking her shoulder.

"God, Val, walk much?"

Val glared up at Sam. "You bumped into...me," her voice stalled out.

The wind blew her hair in front of her face and she scrabbled to get it back behind her ears.

"Sam?" she asked faintly. "What..."

"What?" Sam snapped. "What's the matter with you?"

Val blinked a few times, letting her eyes trail from the top of her sister's head down to her toes and back up again. Words failed her. She'd seen Sam made up plenty of times. Every day before school was a regular fashion and beauty extravaganza but never like this. Never ever like this.

Her eyes were outlined so heavily in kohl that the blue of her irises glowed with an almost preternatural brilliance. Her face was perfectly flawless and smooth and the deep, dark red of her mouth was like a slash of blood across all that paleness. She wore a long, black coat that fell to her ankles. It was cinched tightly at her waist and she loomed over Val even more than usual with the black heels strapped to her feet. The heels were as thin as needles but she teetered on them expertly.

The look on her face wasn't the usual look of triumph or smug knowledge she wore when she *knew* she looked good. It was more of an untouchable domineering glare, kind of like *look but don't touch* or *don't mess with me or I'm gonna stick my heel in your eye*. It was very dramatic, very purposeful and Val suddenly felt very uncomfortable. This wasn't what Sam usually wore when she was going out with her friends.

"Sam? Where are you going?"

"I'll be back in an hour," she stated. She started off down the stairs, heels clacking painfully on the cement.

Val stared blankly after her then shook her head as if coming out of a trance. "Wait! You're still grounded. You can't—"

"I said I'll be back in an hour."

"Do Mom and Dad know—"

"No, they don't and you'd better keep your mouth shut," she said over her shoulder.

"But—"

Sam walked away without another word. The wind blew hard, lifting the ends of her coat to expose her bare legs a little above the knee.

Val felt her insides freeze at the sight of all that bareness. Something tight and weird settled in her gut as she watched Sam strut down the block and then slide into a gold-colored SUV that was idling at the curb.

Any lingering hope of trying to stay away from this was blown away like dead leaves in the wind. Turning slowly as if she were stuck in a giant barrel of pancake syrup, Val went inside. Her brain buzzed loudly and she felt winded even before she started climbing the staircase to her apartment.

Where was Sam going? Who was in that car? Why was she dressed like that?

Val went inside, closed the front door behind her, and leaned stiffly against it. It was no wonder Sam had gone. Dad was at some kind of unemployment meeting and those always took hours because there were so many people trying to make ends meet. Mom wouldn't be home from the bakery until well after dinner.

'I'll be back in an hour.'

Val chewed viciously on her lip until she tasted blood. She went into the kitchen and looked at the clock on the stove. Sinking into a chair at the table, she didn't want to move or breathe until the hour was up. Her palms were hot and sweaty, her clothes stuck to her skin. It was weird feeling this way. Normally she got like this if she had an oral presentation. The only thing missing now was the overwhelming urge to puke. In its place were her thoughts, too tangled, too loud, too confusing for any puking to be involved.

Her eyes remained on the clock. Her knee bounced. This was going to be the day when her parents would come home early. She knew it. She could feel it in her bones.

When that hour came and went and there was no Sam, only their Dad walking through the door, the urge to puke was abruptly in the forefront of her mind. It took all of her willpower to choke it back down.

"Hey there." Her father started to smile but it stopped halfway across his face. "Val? Val, what is it? Are you all right?"

"Yeah," she tried to say but her voice stuck in her throat.

He put a hand on her shoulder then on her cold, sweaty forehead. "You're soaked."

"I'm okay, really."

"What—"

Someone gasped and there was a muted click of a heel on the floor. He turned. Val leaned sideways in her chair to peer around him.

Sam stood in the doorway, immobile, like the universal deer caught in the headlights.

Val's eyes widened. Some kind of strangled sound came out of her throat and astonishment ripped through her like a lightning bolt.

Sam had been eerily gorgeous when she left but coming back in, she looked like she'd been mauled by a bear. Her hair was flat and run through. The dark kohl around her eyes was still there but the carefully-drawn lines were smudged as if they'd run then dried again, making her eyes as big as a raccoon's.

The dark red lipstick was a distant memory but traces of it were smeared around her mouth like she'd wiped a hand over her lips without thinking. Her coat was half-on and Val was able to see clearly that the outfit she wore was hardly an outfit at all. It was a piece of shiny, black fabric that looked like it'd been poured on. Strapless and sleeveless, it barely contained her breasts and it came down to a stop just below her groin. Her knees were red and raw and there was something black and blue—bruises— decorating her left shoulder. God, it looked like a handprint.

Val stared, speechless and stunned. Even her brain was blank.

"Sam?" Dad said, shock coloring his voice.

At the sound of her name, Sam quickly drew her coat all the way around her.

"What the hell are you wearing..." His voice trailed off.

Sam's eyes flicked back and forth between him and Val. Her lips moved soundlessly before she pressed them together. For a second, Val thought she was going to cry.

Her chin quivered and she swallowed hard as if trying to stop a scream from erupting from her throat.

As if a switch was thrown, her face smoothed out and she squared her shoulders. An eyebrow lifted sardonically. "It's called a dress, Dad."

Then the shit hit the fan.

CHAPTER 12

The last time Val saw her father this pissed off was the last time Sam snuck out and that was approximately four weeks ago. At the first sign of smoke coming out of his ears, Val usually hightailed it to her room. This time, however, she was paralyzed. The finger-shaped bruises on Sam's left shoulder felt like a huge hand on her own shoulder, cementing her in place. The air pressure seemed to skyrocket, squeezing her head until she thought it would burst like a grape. But she couldn't move. As much as she wanted to, she just couldn't. Her father's ranting and raving was like low background music. Every now and then a few words would make their way through the fog in her head.

"...irresponsible..."

"...reckless..."

"...leaving the house dressed like that! You must be out of your mind..."

But there was another word that was struggling to punch through Val's mind and the harder she tried to avoid it, the more momentum and speed the word gained until it tore through with all the chaos of a battering ram.

Prosti—

No!

There was *no way.* There was *no* possible way Sam would sink so low. There would be no reason for it. She wouldn't allow it. She wouldn't let anyone have that kind of control over her. Even with the coat hiding the bruise, Val could still feel it glaring at her, snide and contradictory, its presence bright and impossible to ignore. Bile worked up the back of her throat. She gulped until she was sure it would stay down.

"Dad, come *on*, you are not going to walk me to and from school," Sam was saying hotly.

"You're damn right I am!" he bellowed. "I'm going to be on your ass like white on rice!"

Sam managed to look stricken and angry at the same time, each emotion warring for dominance on her face. "That's ridiculous! I have friends—"

"Who don't care anymore about the rules than you do!" Her father cut her off. "I'm not working right now. I might as well put myself to good use."

"Dad—"

"I'll drop you off and I'll be there when the last bell rings."

"Do you have any idea how embarrassing this is going to be?" Sam practically shrieked. "I have a life! I have friends! I'm not some loser geek like Val."

"I don't really care how popular you are. Maybe if you actually applied yourself the way Val does, we wouldn't even be having this conversation."

"You can't do this!"

"Watch me!"

Sam stared at him, her chest heaving. Her eyes moved restlessly over her father, over Val, over the rest of the room, as if searching for something to say, something that would undo this. After a moment, she seemed to give up and flew from the room, moving surprisingly well in the shoes she wore.

Val's breath shot out of her lungs and she found that she could move again. Her father snatched up the phone, fingers flying over the numbers. Val could see that he was dialing the bakery.

Calling for reinforcements.

She got up slowly from the chair and made her way to her own room. Round two was going to be underway when their mother came home.

Val sank down on her bed. She should've said something at the bakery. Maybe then her mother would've come home with her, seen Sam and promptly stopped her from leaving. And perhaps found out what was going on.

Val's head pounded under the strain of what was unfolding. Exhaustion swept over her and she didn't bother stopping herself from dozing as she sank further into the mattress.

Suddenly the sound of running feet nudged her back to awareness. It was followed by rapid, impatient knocking. She stood and stuck her head out into the hallway just in time to see Justin disappear into Sam's room. The door swung shut behind him but it didn't latch. By some misalignment of door hinges or a strange sloping of the apartment floorboards, the door slowly swung back open. Val stared at it. Distantly she could hear her father in the kitchen, still on the phone.

Forget it, she thought as she turned back to her bed.

She decided she really, really needed a nap. But then her little brother's distraught voice floated out to her.

"—did he mean?"

This was followed by a low murmur from Sam, too low for Val to hear the words but the timbre was soothing, calming. But Justin apparently wasn't in the mood to be soothed or calmed.

"—laughed at you. He said you did whatever they said, like a dog. A dog, Sam! He said he should've made a video and put it on *YouTube*!"

Frowning, Val went silently down the hall, stopping a few feet from Sam's door.

"—just a joke," Sam was saying.

"No, it wasn't," Justin replied in a shaky voice.

Val knew he was close to tears. He always teared up when he was angry.

"Justin, if I said it was a joke, it was a joke. Ryan's older brother is a jerk. You've said it yourself lots of times."

There was a small pause, followed by sniffling. Val chewed on her lip. Justin and Ryan have been friends since kindergarten. They were close, sharing many things including the same slightly insane obsession with comic books. Ryan's older brother, Brandon, was a senior in high school. He was the star pitcher of the baseball team and easily one of the biggest jackasses Val ever had the displeasure of knowing. He and Sam had tried dating last year—which was a disaster from the start. Between Sam's independence and Brandon's possessiveness, not to mention his teeth-gritting habit of calling Sam his "little kitten," the relationship broke apart after only six weeks. If Sam was telling the story, she kicked Brandon to the curb. If Brandon was telling the story, he kicked her to the curb. Val had rolled her eyes so much she was surprised they didn't get stuck.

Could he still be harboring a grudge after all this time? Is that why he got Justin so upset? For some kind of belated revenge?

"It wasn't a joke and he wasn't lying," Justin insisted in that whining, pleading voice that only kids could pull off without sounding ridiculous.

"Justin—"

"No!" he cut in, his voice thick. "No. He laughed at me. Him and all his stupid friends. They just laughed and then I just ran home. I—"

"It's not a big deal," Sam said, obviously trying to be firm and gentle at the same time.

Val could hear her words tremble around the edges. She chewed on her fingernail, her heart already setting a too-fast pace in her chest.

"They'll laugh about it now and probably tomorrow but after that, they'll be laughing about something else. They're just stupid, Justin. Stupid and mean. You know that."

"Did you do it?" Justin demanded. "All the things that they said? Did you do any of it?"

Val held her breath. Endless minutes ticked by until Sam said so softly Val almost didn't hear her. "No, Justin. I didn't. Okay?"

Justin let out a noise that was half a frustrated sigh and half a sob. He ran from the room, nearly knocking Val over. He went into their bedroom and slammed the door.

Val stayed put, even though she realized that she'd better get her ass out of there before Sam decided to follow him. But she heard no movement from inside her room. Moving slowly, Val eased herself forward and peeked inside.

Sam was perched on the edge of her bed, dressed in sweatpants and a large T-shirt now. The dress she'd worn was crumpled in the far corner as if it'd been thrown there. Val stared at the small hopeless picture that Sam made. Hunched in on herself, her hands in her hair, crying silently, choking on the misery that was so plainly written across her pretty face.

CHAPTER 13

Val's father was true to his word. The next morning he marched Sam to school like a prison warden. Everyone gawked and laughed. Sam's jaw tightened so hard it threatened to snap off her face. She held her head high, not looking at anyone as she moved through the crowds.

Val felt as if she'd dreamt the entire thing. Her sister's disheveled appearance, the conversation between her and Justin, seeing her cry so hopelessly—it was like nothing had ever happened as Sam breezed through the apartment this morning, meticulously made up and looking as fabulous and *Vogue*-worthy as ever. Her smug, indifferent mask was securely in place, and it left Val frustrated and even more confused as she made her way to her locker.

She felt like she was in pieces—like the pieces of a broken vase swept up and put inside a brown paper bag. All there, but completely damaged. The crowded echoing wave of noise and chatter around her was deafening and muted all at once. The lights in the ceiling blazed too brightly, illuminating wild rolling eyes, wide, gaping mouths, and flailing limbs. God, it was like being in the midst of stampeding, carnivorous beasts. She spun the combination on her locker and opened it. The cool darkness inside was inviting and if she could fit, she would've climbed in.

"Hey," someone said from beside her.

Startled out her haze, she turned. Allison stood in front of her, smiling tentatively as if she wasn't sure if she should be there. Val blinked at her, deciding that, no, she shouldn't be there. Without a word, she turned back to her locker, starting to go through her stack of books that she would need for the first four periods of the day.

"How've you been?" Allison asked.

"Fine."

Allison shifted her weight. "I saw your mom the other day. At the bakery."

Val shot her a look. "Was that before you ignored me and took off down the street with Julia?"

Allison winced. "Uh, about that—"

"Yeah, about that," Val said sharply. "How long did you have to listen to her complain about the fact that there were no blueberry muffins?"

"Nearly an hour," Allison grumbled, her cheeks turning pink.

"Serves you right."

"Val, come on. I'm just trying to—"

"What?" Val cut in, feeling all her emotions boil to the surface. "What're you trying to do?"

"I didn't mean to do what I did, okay? I just needed some time—"

"Time? Time for what?"

Allison raised an eyebrow. "You know what."

"And you couldn't tell me that?"

"It's...I...It's complicated."

"No, it isn't. We were friends, Allison or at least, I thought we were. If you needed space or time or someone to talk to or whatever, you could've just said so."

"You have no idea what I've been through."

"And you have no idea what *I've* been through. I thought we were friends. I thought...I don't know and then suddenly you didn't want to be friends anymore and there were no explanations."

Allison flexed her jaw. "I know. God, don't you think I know what I did?"

"I don't think you have the slightest idea. So what happened, huh? What changed that would you start talking to me again? Or did you just get tired of hanging out with Julia too?"

"This has nothing to do with her."

"Yes, it does. Does she know that this is how you treat your friends? Does she know that you just start pretending they don't exist for no reason at all?"

Allison fidgeted, her fingers clasping and unclasping around her book bag strap. Val got the impression that Allison was thinking that this wasn't going the way she'd hoped.

Val felt a strange surge of glee. *Good.*

"Val, I think you're being over dramatic."

That stung. Val stared at her, shocked and angry that Allison would wrangle this into something so small, that Val was somehow being unreasonable. A wave of anger so potent and foreign completely enveloped her. It was thick and suffocating and it sparked real fear in Val because she never got mad about anything. She got aggravated, she got annoyed, frustrated, irritated, irked, but full out angry? She left that to Sam. But now, at this very moment, with so many things in tatters and pocked with holes and uncertainty, in this new and unforgiving light in which she was being forced to see things for the first time, Val let the anger wash over her.

She leaned into Allison and said, "And I think you're being a bitch."

Allison's eyes went wide. She moved back a step as if Val had pushed her.

Val turned away from her, feeling her body shake with tiny tremors as she stared unseeingly at her books in her locker. She heard Allison move away from her, vaguely noticing that her stride was almost back to normal now. She felt her throat tighten and her eyeballs burned.

Oh God, don't cry. Come on, get a grip. She deserved it. You know she did. After everything she put you through? She deserved worse than that. You let her off easy.

She gripped her locker door, the edges biting into her fingers. She realized after a moment that she was breathing like she just ran a marathon. Trying to curb it, she hung her head, wondering when the feeling of vindication was going to present itself.

She had stood up for herself. Wouldn't everyone be proud? Wouldn't everyone be shocked? There should be a parade. There should be a holiday. Classes should be cancelled. There should be fanfare and confetti, not this gaping black hole in the center of her chest. Val groaned to herself, wanting nothing more than to melt into the floor.

"Valerie! What's up, girl?"

She jumped and turned at the booming voice that battered her eardrums.

Sam's-my-little-kitten-Brandon leaned a shoulder on the locker next to hers, bending over her like some giant willow tree. She automatically leaned away from him, her eyes watering on the gagging, too much scent of his cologne.

On a good day when her brain unknowingly relapsed, she could see why Sam went out with him even if it was for only six weeks. He was tall and lean with enough muscle definition that he showed off with tight shirts and low-slung jeans. Blond-haired, brown-eyed, all-American— except when he opened his mouth. He had a smile like a shark and once he smelled blood in the water, he was mean and relentless. In all the years that Justin and Ryan had known each other, and their families have grown relatively close and familiar, Brandon never once spoke willingly to Val. Now here he was in her face with no obvious knowledge of personal space.

"What's up?" she said hesitantly.

His shark smile stretched across his face. Val felt the hairs on the back of her neck rise up in warning. "Your brother all right?"

Her jaw tightened, remembering Justin's angry, tear-choked voice. He'd gone to bed without speaking to anyone. He'd skipped supper, too.

"He's fine," she said tightly.

"You sure?

"Yeah."

"He was pretty upset when he left my house yesterday."

He rubbed at his jaw, grinning smugly at her. Val's vision tunneled on the sight of his hand. Her eyes followed its back and forth motion as if suddenly hypnotized.

Were his fingers the ones that had left their mark on Sam's shoulder? Was he the one who'd grabbed her, letting his fingers bite into her flesh like she was some kind of...oh God, she couldn't even—

Val broke away from the thought, her heart shuddering in her rib cage. "I don't know what you're talking about," she managed to say in a steady voice.

Brandon's hand dropped to his belt. "Oh, sure you do, sweetheart."

"No, I really don't, and don't call me that."

He chuckled, low and dark. He moved closer until she could feel his breath on her face. She stayed frozen in place, half-wishing Allison was still with her.

Oh my God, her mind raced. *Oh my God, what is he doing?*

His closeness was like ice down her spine and she didn't like it at all. She gave a quick glance around the hallway. It was crowded, teeming with people but she felt somehow alone, that Brandon would be able to do whatever he wanted and get away with it.

"You don't like it? Your sister does."

Something crawled through her veins at the mention of Sam. It was a rush of protectiveness that she never felt before and it was tinged with a desperation that was almost painful. For a brief second, it confused her, sent her thoughts upside down and around, but then an image came into her mind. An image of her sister perched on her bed with the hopeless sag of her shoulders and the fear in her voice as she spoke in the darkness of a late-night phone call. It was a side so well-hidden behind the taunts, the ridicules, and the mockery that it made Val afraid to think of how long it had been going on and how blind she'd been to it.

That simple fact alone served to invoke a strong sense of hunger for answers. She needed to get to the bottom of Sam's desolation. She wasn't sure if Sam would ever do the same for her—if Sam would ever *feel* the same sense of need, but Val knew herself and she had to do this. It was important and as her sister, as her family, bonded by flesh and blood, no matter how much she and Sam had tried to argue otherwise, it was a responsibility. Sam needed to know that she wasn't alone. She needed to know that someone could and would go to the wall for her.

With this newfound purpose and determination, Val fixed Brandon with a hard stare. "So what if she does? Does that mean I have to like it too?"

"Well, why not?" he shrugged, flashing his shark smile once more. "It'd be double the fun."

The wave of anger that had receded from her conversation with Allison suddenly came back with a roar. She slammed her locker shut. "Is there a point to this conversation?"

"Oh, feisty. Least now I know it runs in the family."

"You don't know anything about my family."

"I don't? Really? Our brothers have been friends for a few years now. I dated your sister for a while. I think I know *some* things about your family."

"You call six weeks a while?"

"When it comes to Sam, six weeks is a lifelong commitment."

"And what about your track record?"

He grinned. "I've never had any complaints."

"Not to your face."

His eyes narrowed. "You want to find out, Valerie?"

He let his fingers travel lightly down the back of her arm. Goosebumps popped up and it wasn't the good kind either. She yanked her arm away. "Would you be offended if I said *no way in hell?*"

The smug look on his face faded but didn't drop completely. "You should try everything at least once," he offered.

"Wise words."

"Sam knows all about that, you know. She's given *everyone* a try, at least once." The smile he gave her was nasty and suggestive.

The back of Val's neck went hot. "That's slander and you're disgusting."

He laughed. "Why don't you talk to your sister about the things *she* does before you call *me* disgusting?"

Val's jaw tightened. She forced herself to breath evenly. The wheels in her head were turning, gearing up and she had to act quickly. "And what kinds of things does she do?"

"What, like you don't know?"

"I wouldn't be standing here listening to this garbage if I did."

"Garbage? You think I'm lying? I *know* you probably saw her in that easily-accessible dress yesterday."

"Apparently you did, too. You are aware that she's a minor, right?"

He scoffed. "Like that matters."

"No?" Val said with raised eyebrows. "She's only seventeen. You're eighteen, aren't you?"

A strange look came over his face. "We went out last year."

"You were both minors then."

The humor was gone from his face now and he straightened away from the lockers to glare down at her. "I never said I did anything."

Gotcha. "You saw her in that dress. *Easily accessible* I think you called it. Now how would you know that if you didn't do anything?"

His lips twisted and he glanced over his shoulder as if to see if anyone was eavesdropping. "Just because I saw her doesn't mean I did anything—"

"I'm sure my brother can recall the things you said you did to her, especially after he came home in tears."

Brandon blinked at her, going very still. She suspected that he was beginning to regret coming over to her. When he spoke again, his voice was as hard as stone. "I didn't do anything."

"You sure?" she parroted back to him. "There's a nice bruise on her shoulder. I wonder if it matches your hand."

He was suddenly moving forward as if someone had shoved him. He forced her back against the lockers. Val sucked in a sharp breath, staring up at him, at the rage that trembled beneath his features. She swallowed hard, determined to stay in control.

"She wanted it," he hissed, his eyes burning. "She wanted it all. He said we could do whatever we wanted and we did. We didn't hear any complaints from her."

Val swallowed hard, feeling on the verge of something big, something that sent her heart rate skyrocketing through the roof.

"Who was it?"

"What?"

"You said 'he'. Who's he?"

"The guy she came with."

"Who was he?" she insisted.

"How the hell am I supposed to know?"

"Tell me who he is!" It came out desperate and loud, causing some people nearby to stop and stare.

"Listen, bitch—"

Brandon was suddenly ripped back away from her. His words ended in a yelp as he was slammed back into the lockers. Val flinched in surprise then gaped when she saw John inches away from Brandon, effortlessly pinning him to the lockers.

"What's up, man?" John greeted him casually, his voice quiet and rumbling.

The muscles in his forearms bunched as he clenched his fists into Brandon's shirt. Brandon stared down at him in shock, his face turning bright red as the air was yanked from his lungs. He looked as surprised to see John as Val was. A crowd had gathered around them, murmuring and enraptured by the possibility of a fight this early in the morning.

"N—Nothing. Nothing's up," Brandon stammered hoarsely.

He towered over John by at least half a foot but John had bulk to his advantage and he used it. His gaze was steady and intense upon Brandon's face. He seemed oblivious to the fact that they had an audience but Val knew that he didn't care about stuff like that. John did what John wanted to do, and the quiet confidence he exuded either made people listen or get the hell out of his way.

In a school full of wanna-bes and imposters, he was the real deal. But he wasn't a trouble maker despite the rumors that circled constantly about the jail time he supposedly did and the gun he supposedly carried. According to Sam, he'd never been in jail and he'd never fired a gun in his life. Although looking at him, sometimes one had to wonder. Between the bandana around his head and the baggy clothes, he could definitely pass as a gang-banger or a felon or both. But John was smart. He hardly ever got into trouble and when he did, it was usually to help someone else out.

Like now.

But as much as Val appreciated his intentions, she didn't want or need it. She was just starting to get some answers, and now that John was here, she doubted she was going to get any more information.

"Wait," she said. "John, wait—"

"Yeah? You seem pretty riled up about something," he said, talking over her, still in Brandon's face.

"It's not—" she tried to say but Brandon was shaking his head, his eyes wide.

"No," Brandon said. "No, I'm—it's all good, man."

John stared silently at him for a few moments then he slowly released Brandon's shirt. He didn't move away, forcing Brandon to squeeze by him before taking off down the hall. Shoulders sagging, Val watched him disappear around the corner.

Crap.

"Aw man, that's it?" someone said from the crowd.

Groans of disappointment rose from the onlookers but they were quickly silenced by John's glare as he turned around. Val was disappointed herself but for an entirely different reason. She shook her head before looking up at him. His pale green eyes shone brightly, the dark lashes framing them made them glow like they were lit from within. On any other day, she would've stammered and blushed and then run away from him. But today things were spiraling out of control and instead of embarrassment. She faced him with the frustration of having been denied, of having something within her grasp and then having it yanked away at the last minute. Oddly enough, it made her think of her softball game when she'd hit the triple, and Kenny, the smug pain-in-her-ass, had called her out even though she and everybody else knew that she was safe.

So close, so close but not close enough.

She balled her hands into fists. She watched as the crowd split up then turned to John. "It was fine," she snapped. "You didn't have to do that."

He raised an eyebrow at her. "Didn't look fine."

"Well, it was. We were just talking."

"That wasn't talking."

"How would you know?"

He stared quietly down at her. "That wasn't talking."

She shook her head again, her frustration growing. "Whatever. I've got to go."

He stepped in front of her, blocking her way. She looked up at him in surprise.

"Everything all right?"

"It was fine until you butted in."

"Brandon's no good. You got no business talking to him."

"Excuse me?" she said incredulously.

"I'm just saying."

"Well, don't. I can take care of myself."

He cocked his head at her as he slipped his hands inside the pockets of his jeans. He seemed so calm in the face of her anger that it was beginning to make her feel stupid. She took a few deep breaths, trying to settle down but it was hard. The irony of this situation wasn't lost on her either. Her first conversation with John, just the two of them, and it wasn't even a pleasant one.

Allison would find this hysterical. She gave herself a mental shake then raised her chin. "Look, I appreciate your...whatever, but it wasn't needed, okay?"

He continued to look at her, as if trying to see into her brain. She glanced away, feeling like an ant under a magnifying glass.

He shrugged. "Okay."

"Don't tell Sam."

His lips quirked. "About what?"

"About me talking to Brandon."

He dipped his head, giving her a look like she'd done something cute. She felt her face grow hot. "I don't think she's gonna hear it from me."

Val sighed. "Yeah."

Prepare yourself for another ass-reaming.

Then she had an idea.

"John, can I, uh, can I ask you something?"

"Of course."

He moved closer to her, his eyes intent upon her face. It was as if the rest of the world had fallen away and she was the only thing he was focused on. At least that was what she liked to think. It was a nice thought too. She took a deep breath, smelling his cologne that was so much sweeter and subtler than Brandon's. It made her lean forward a bit before she caught herself.

She cleared her throat. "Look, about Sam—"

"What about her?" he said immediately, concerned.

Val could only wish for friends as loyal as him. She was about to say, *I think she's in trouble*, when Audrey and Bryan came around the corner.

"Hey, hey!"

"Yo, John!

John turned and took a step back so that he was at Val's side instead of standing in front of her. She saw Audrey's step falter when she saw her. The corners of her mouth turned down a little.

"Hey Val, what's up?"

"Heard your dad's playing prison warden," Bryan said with a chuckle as he slung an arm around Audrey's neck.

Val shrugged, not saying anything. She noticed Audrey giving her a sly look and knew that her conversation with Brandon wasn't going to be the only thing that Sam heard about today. She glanced away.

"How long is that gonna go on for?" Bryan smirked.

"Till he finds a job probably," Audrey said.

"Hope he finds one soon. Did you see the look on Sam's face when she came into school today?"

"Don't suppose you'd look any different if *your* dad walked *you* to school," John said.

"My old man doesn't even know where the school is."

"My dad doesn't walk anywhere," Audrey chimed in. "He'd probably drive me though if he was that pissed off at me. Why's your dad so pissed off at Sam, Val?

Val looked at her, surprised. "You don't know?"

"Haven't had a chance to talk to her yet."

Suddenly Val didn't want to be here. She started to back away, clutching at the strap of her book bag.

"Dude, where are you going?" Audrey demanded.

"I've got class," Val stammered out.

"Yeah well, tell your dad to stop being a dick," Bryan called after her.

Val ignored him, shooting John a quick look. He was looking at her with a calculating gleam in his eyes. She turned away and went quickly down the hallway, feeling him watching her the whole way.

CHAPTER 14

The rest of the day completely and utterly sucked. There wasn't a moment to breathe between the stupid rumors and the stupid questions and the *stupid* people starting all the rumors and asking all the questions. High school was one big gob of stupidity. Val couldn't believe that there were people who actually believed that she and Brandon had gotten into a fight. An actual brawl, with fists being thrown, blood being shed, and hair being pulled.

Seriously? Where did people, who were supposed to be her peers, even come up with this stuff?

Not even John could escape the wheels of gossip. He was playing the part of white knight, riding to her rescue when she'd apparently been a hair-width away from getting her face kicked in. She wondered if he found it as ridiculous as she did. Perhaps what was even more troubling than John playing the hero was the fact that even though Brandon supposedly used her as a punching bag, there were a tremendous amount of people on his side, as if she had somehow deserved getting knocked around. Her lack of bruises certainly added a level of falsity to the rumors but it was still disturbing how many dirty looks she received and how many taunts had been thrown her way.

Popularity at its finest, she thought miserably.

Sneaking her lunch into the library, Val was able to get at least forty-five minutes of peace and quiet to analyze what she found out from Brandon. It didn't bring her any closer to finding out what was going on with Sam, but she was convinced that someone was forcing Sam to do these things—forcing her to wear a dress that barely covered her body, forcing her on her knees to do unspeakable things to jerkwads like Brandon and his meathead friends. And even if, as Brandon said, she didn't complain, it didn't mean that she wanted to do it. Not that that mattered. Brandon wasn't exactly the type to turn down an opportunity to get laid. Like any guy would. More than half probably couldn't tell the difference between a chick who was enjoying herself and one who wasn't.

Just look at *When Harry Met Sally*. Perfect example in the diner scene when Harry insisted that he knew when a woman was faking it. Guys had no idea, and Sam was a pretty good actress, too.

Val's stomach churned at the thought of what her sister was going through. The question was, why? Why was she doing it? And second of all, who was the guy who took her to these little get-togethers? What kind of pull did he have over her to make her do these things? Was he blackmailing her? Was he threatening to kill her, or maybe Mom and Dad, if she didn't comply with his demands?

It was like something out of a bad movie and Val really, really wanted to change the channel.

Finally the last bell of the day rang. She waded through the crowds of students. Near the school's front steps, she caught sight of John, Bryan, Audrey and Sam.

And Sam was looking directly at her.

Val nearly tripped and went face first but she caught herself. She looked behind her, wondering if there was someone else who'd caught her sister's attention.

But no.

Sam was staring at *her*, ignoring the exuberant story that Bryan was telling, complete with flailing limbs and probably more curses than actual words. Even from where she stood, Val could feel the weight of her stare. Students and teachers alike wove in the space between them, shielding her from Sam's sight then unveiling her like the sun moving in and out from behind the clouds and still, Sam's gaze never wavered, never flinched.

Her face was a stone mask but Val could feel the movement beneath it. Not for the first time she wondered if any of this was a good idea. She wondered if what she was doing was going to actually help Sam instead of damaging or hindering her in some awful way that Val tried not to think about. A strange heaviness settled onto her shoulders, and as she stared at her sister, the sad truth that so much more than space separated them was made so apparent and obvious that Val knew she didn't have a choice but to see this through. There was no going back now.

Val broke the staring contest, turning away and heading home. She saw her father waiting for Sam at the curb, and as Sam begrudgingly made her way towards him, the laughter that followed her echoed up and down the street. At that moment, Val was struck by the extremely good fortune that of all the stupid "reasons" that she and Brandon had "fought," the *real* reason behind the conversation was never brought to light. If it had been, there'd be a lot more than laughter following Sam home.

She followed them home, taking care to stay far back, not wanting to be seen. It had nothing to do with the embarrassment of being seen with her father out in public. She just didn't want to be around Sam. Val knew that sooner or later Sam was going to corner her and the longer Val could put that little get-together off, the better. She didn't have all the information she needed to make a solid argument yet and she had no intention of telling Sam anything anyway. Sam was only going to deny it. So Val was going to go straight to their parents. She was going to take everything she knew, everything she found out and present it to Mom and Dad and if the cops had to be called and arrests had to be made, then so be it. At least Sam would be safe and away from whoever was making her do these things.

'*She wanted it. She wanted it all.*'

Brandon's words reverberated through her mind. She didn't believe it for a minute and she didn't think Brandon believed it either. Or maybe he was just really good at denial.

Arriving home, Val said hello to her father then quickly and quietly made her way towards her bedroom. Sam's door was shut. Val all but leapt past it. Sam probably heard the floorboards creak as she went by but her door remained closed. Breathing a sigh of relief, Val hurried into her room and closed the door.

A hand grabbed her shoulder and spun her around.

She bit back a scream. Her book bag thudded to the floor.

Sam pressed her back against the door, fingers digging hard into her shoulder.

"Sam!" Val gaped at her. "What—"

"Shhh!" Sam shushed her with a hard look.

Val closed her mouth with a *click*. She stared up at her sister, wondering how many bones in her face would be broken by the time Sam was done with her.

"What do you think you're doing, Valerie?" Sam demanded, her voice quiet and measured.

Sam calling her by her full name caught Val off guard. "Nothing. I mean, what?" she stammered.

"Valerie," she said, a warning clear in her tone.

"I—"

"Don't bother lying. It's all over school."

"What, that thing with Brandon?"

Sam gave her a look as if to say "duh." Val tried to make herself slump nonchalantly against the door.

"He's a jackass. It was nothing."

Sam tried to drill holes into Val's head with her eyes. Her lack of anger was surprising but that usually meant she was going to keep Val trapped until she told her everything. This wasn't looking very good.

"John doesn't agree," Sam said.

Val felt her face redden. "It was none of John's business. Brandon and I were just talking. No big deal."

Sam slammed her palm into the door, inches from Val's head. Val jumped, making a strange squeaking sound as Sam leaned in close. There was still no anger, just an icy calmness that set Val's already-fraying nerves on edge. "*What* were you talking to Brandon about?"

Val swallowed hard. She wasn't going to be able to tap dance her way out of this one. She bought her hands up in surrender. "Okay, okay. Just don't kill me."

Sam raised an eyebrow.

Val licked her dry lips. "We were talking about Justin."

Sam blinked in surprise, leaning back a little. "Justin?"

"Yeah. You know how he came home crying the other day? From Ryan and Brandon's house?"

Sam's lips parted like she wanted to say something. She sucked in a sharp breath instead, the look in her eyes slowing changing from hole-drilling to searching. Raising her chin, she looked down her nose at Val. "He did?"

Val looked back at her. *So I guess she's going to play stupid now.* "Yeah. He went into your room."

The grip on Val's shoulder abruptly slackened but Sam kept her hand there. She skinned her top lip over her teeth and gave a small jerk of her head. When she spoke, her voice was low and hesitant as if she wasn't sure what she should be saying. "No, he didn't."

Val thrust her head forward like a turtle, forcing Sam to keep eye contact. "Yes, he did."

"*No*, he didn't."

"Sam, I heard him. I heard him in your room."

Her eyes widened. The blood left her face. "You were listening?"

"It was kind of hard not to—wait, what're you doing, ow!"

Sam tugged hard on her arm, trying to pull her away from the door. "Get the hell out of the way."

Val dug her heels in. "Hey, hang on a second. I—"

"I can't believe you were listening," Sam growled at her, her face pale and tight with anger now. But the anger seemed forced like she wasn't really angry but felt like she had to be, on principle.

"Oh, come on. I heard Justin crying. I was worried—"

"Bullshit!" Sam snapped. "You were being nosy, as usual, sticking your face into my business *again*."

She tossed Val's arm away as if it offended her. She moved in close, getting her hand around the doorknob while trying to shoulder-shove Val out of the way. Val strained against her.

"I wasn't trying to be nosy. Justin—"

"He wasn't crying. He wasn't even in my room."

"When are you gonna stop lying?"

"I'm not lying! Dammit, Val, since when do you even give a crap about what I do?" Sam exclaimed.

Do it. Just do it. Show her that you know. Show her that you're here to help.

Val stared up at her and set her jaw before grabbing at Sam's shirt.

"Hey! Are you crazy or something? Get off me!"

Pulling down hard on Sam's sleeve, the bruised outline of the hand print on her shoulder came to light. It was still dark purple and black in some places, looking as hideous and heart stopping as it did the first time Val saw it. A pained gasp came from Sam's mouth as if Val had punched her in the gut.

"This, Sam. I started giving a crap when I saw this."

Sam went still, twisting her head to look down at her shoulder. Val saw the edge of her jaw move, grinding down until the muscles bulged. She felt her sister tense against her shoulder, so stiff that it was like leaning against a brick wall.

Val waited, holding her breath, uncertain once again if she was doing the right thing. Seconds ticked by, then minutes until it felt like a lifetime that they stood there, leaning awkwardly against one another.

Finally, Sam slowly, so slowly, raised her face. The nastiness that settled there made Val's heart sink and she felt herself shrink under the weight of it.

"Sam—" she tried to say.

Sam shoved her, hard enough that Val had to catch herself against the bureau. Everything on top of it wobbled precariously and her hairbrush clattered to the floor. Jerking her sleeve back up to cover her shoulder, Sam sent her a scathing glare.

"I want to help," Val implored.

Sam laughed but it was humorless and full of rusty nails. "You want to help? With what? What do you think is going on here, Val? What the hell have you concocted inside that big fat brain of yours? Huh? What?"

Val pushed herself away from the bureau. Her knees felt weak beneath the cold but steady pressure of Sam's denial and anger. "You have a handprint on your shoulder."

"Nice observation, Einstein."

"You would never let anyone touch you like that, Sam."

Sam's eyebrows rose mockingly. "Oh really? And you know this for a fact because you know me *so* well, don't you?"

Val took a step towards her. "I saw you in that dress. You looked completely miserable, and you were even more miserable when you came home. You looked like you'd been hit by a truck."

Sam folded her arms across her chest. "Oh please. Of course I wasn't happy when I got home. I got busted by Dad *again*. Are you ever happy when you get grounded? Oh wait, you probably don't even know what that feels like because you're always such a good little girl."

Her sarcasm was like red-hot pokers being swiped dangerously close to her face, hot and foreboding. Val felt her nerves snap at long last.

"Brandon said you wanted it."

The stark silence that followed her words was as ear-piercing as a bomb going off. The look on Sam's face was indescribable—the feeling of being the one to put that look there was even more so. Sam's arms fell to her side, her knuckles sharp and white as she balled her hands into fists. She looked torn between laughing it off, screaming or crying. Each emotion trembled across her face like a blanket whipping in the wind while hanging from a clothesline. And Val wanted to throw her hands up in victory, in hard-won triumph while at the same time, wanting a dark place to hide forever.

Feeling her insides shake and quiver, she took another step forward. Sam stared at her, motionless. Val had to swallow two times to get her voice to work properly. She had Sam in her sights now but did she want to keep her there? "He said you wanted it all," she pushed on. "And that you weren't complaining about any of it."

The taste of bile swam among her words and she forced it down, the horrible feeling in her gut beginning to viciously spread like a thick, coagulated mess. But she had to finish what she started. The avalanche was already too big and too fast for her to put a stop to it.

"He said there was a guy who brought you to the party, who told Brandon that he and his friends could do what they wanted." Her voice cracked alarmingly and she took a deep breath. "God, Sam, what are you mixed up in?"

Sam stared unseeingly at a spot over Val's shoulder as if in a trance.

"Sam, come on. Let me help—"

Sam's eyes suddenly snapped to her face so fast that Val jumped. Her ice-pale eyes seethed with frustrated rage and...fear. Her fingers curled tightly around Val's biceps, giving her a hard shake.

"Don't, Val," she warned. "Don't you dare. If you get involved, I'm dead. We're both dead."

A cold spike of fear shot through Val's rib cage. The triumph of finally knowing for certain that her sister was unwillingly involved in something was vastly undercut by the possibility of danger. And the danger was real and scary. Val had to look no further than Sam's eyes to know that. Hysterically, Val thought of every movie she'd ever seen, every book she'd ever read where the odds are firmly stacked against the hero and there was no way out, no escape. But the hero always used his bravery, his courage to prevail in the end. There was always a moment of clarity, of hope and always, always one small thing that the bad guys had missed and the hero would use that to his advantage and save the day. Val waited for her courage to assail her, waited for the right words that she could say that would fix everything, that would give Sam hope and not fear.

She waited.

And waited.

But all that was there was fear.

Cold and paralyzing.

Along with the dawning knowledge that this was bigger than both of them.

A lot bigger.

"We...the police," Val said weakly.

"No." Sam's fingers tightened like claws on her arms.

Val winced.

"No cops, no telling Mom and Dad, no telling anyone. It's bad enough that you know."

"But I—"

"Val—"

"I want to help you, Sam, please. You can't keep this up. Mom and Dad will find out eventually and—"

"No, they won't. They've got enough to worry about."

That struck Val as odd. She gave her sister a strange look. "What, you don't—you don't think they'd *care* about something like this?"

"I didn't say that."

"Are you out of your mind? Of course they—"

Sam clamped a hand over her mouth, pushing her backwards until Val felt the wall behind her.

"Shut up," Sam whispered sharply with a shake of her head. "Geez." She blew out a long breath.

Val still tried to talk though her words were muffled and in her aggravation of not being heard, she began to struggle.

Sam pinned her effortlessly to the wall. "Stop it," she murmured. "Val, stop."

Val tried to shake her head but Sam's hand was tight on her face. She seemed almost calm now, in control once again and that was scarier now than her being angry. Sam being calm meant reasonable and there was nothing reasonable about this situation. Defeated, Val slumped against the wall.

"Look, I know this sucks," Sam explained. "Okay, I know, but it's not going to last. It's not," she repeated when

Val tried to speak again. "You're just going to have to trust me."

Val tugged at Sam's wrist. She uncovered Val's mouth with a roll of her eyes.

"How—" she stopped and lowered her voice. "How do you expect me *not* to say anything when I know what you're being forced to do?"

"Who says I'm being forced?"

Val's eyes went wide. "You are—"

"Valerie, when has anyone ever forced me to do anything that I didn't want to do?"

But Val was shaking her head even before Sam was finished speaking. "No, no, don't do that."

"Don't do what?"

"Don't act like this is no big deal. Don't act like this is something that you actually want to do!"

"Lame-brain, weren't you listening? Someone will get hurt, namely myself or worse, if I *don't* do this. And as far as not wanting to do it? Okay, maybe not but if I don't act like I want to do it, I'll probably go freaking nuts and slit my wrists out of misery. Now which do you prefer?"

"Neither!"

"Tough shit. You don't get that luxury."

"Sam, please, we'll find a way. The cops will protect you. They'll—"

"Please. The cops? You've been watching way too many *Lifetime* movies."

"I don't like *Lifetime* movies and the cops will help. That's their job."

Sam's eyes turned solemn. "I'll be dead before that can happen."

Val felt like someone just kicked her in the stomach. She stared up at her sister, tried to imagine the life she would have without her in it. Her mind filled with gaping wounds overflowing with devastation, loss, and despair. A yawning black hole broke open before her, far enough away but still too close, waiting, waiting. With something between a gasp and a cry, she clutched at Sam's arms but Sam untangled herself quickly as if sensing what was going through Val's mind. She moved towards the door. Val's hands hung uselessly in midair.

"Sam..."

Sam gave her a small smile over her shoulder. "I know you want to help, Val. I'm kind of surprised by it, actually. But you couldn't have picked a worse time to start caring."

She left the room, closing the door quietly behind her.

Val's knees gave out and she slid down to the floor. Helplessness crashed over her. She found herself staring into that yawning black hole, the edges crumbling, coming closer to the toes of her sneakers, seeking her out. She knew it would only be a matter of time before she fell in.

CHAPTER 15

Getting through the day was bad enough but the nights were even worse. Plagued by nightmares that left her shaking and soaked in sweat, Val could only lay in bed, wide eyed and staring up at the ceiling until her eyelids fell closed on their own. Minutes later, she would snap awake, heart pounding, swearing she could see a dark figure standing in the corner of her room. It was a miracle Justin never woke up.

She couldn't look Sam in the eye anymore. Sam seemed to realize that and went out of her way to avoid her, never speaking to her, never so much as being in the same room if she could possibly help it.

It was even harder putting on a smiling face in front of their parents. So Val solved that problem by staying late at school, in the library, burying herself in homework and trying not to think. And on days when she had a softball game, she would arrive hours early to practice and not leave until the field lights were shut off.

It was constantly on the tip of her tongue to tell their parents what was going on. The urge to *unload* was mounting with each passing day until Val thought she would be permanently hunched over beneath the weight of it. It wasn't long before she began to resent both herself and Sam as well. She kicked herself daily for getting involved, for giving a crap when Sam so obviously didn't, when Sam was the one who got into this mess in the first place. But no matter how resentful she got, Val's thoughts kept coming back to Sam's fear of exposure.

'*If you get involved, I'm dead. We're both dead.*'

It frightened the hell out of her. For reasons Val couldn't explain, she believed in that threat a hundred and ten percent and it left her with little else to do than keep quiet—because what could she do? How was she supposed to cope with this? How was *Sam* dealing with this?

Val didn't believe Sam's claim of "It's not going to last." She didn't believe that for a second. No one inspired fear in a person over something that was short term. And there was money involved, too. She hadn't forgotten about that fifty dollar bill that had been sticking out of Sam's back pocket. Money made people do stupid things. It was a lot like being in love, Val figured. It made people brain dead.

Walking home from school, Val ran into Justin coming out of the bakery. He was munching happily on a chocolate muffin the size of a grapefruit. He waved at her. "Hi Val!" he mumbled around a mouth full of pastry.

Val found herself smiling at the sight, the first real smile in what felt like forever. "Hey, little man. How's that muffin treating you?"

"Pretty good."

Val slowed her stride as Justin tried to eat and walk at the same time. "How's Mom doing?" she asked.

"Busy. You want to go back and—"

"No, no, it's okay. Got some homework I need to get started on."

Justin wiped at his mouth, smearing chocolate and crumbs across his cheek. Val rolled her eyes and dug a tissue out of her book bag.

"Napkins, Justin. They were invented for a reason."

"It's more fun this way," he said, but he took the tissue anyway.

"And messy."

"That's because you're a girl."

"Thanks for noticing."

"Girls are always worried about getting dirty."

"Unlike you."

"That's because I'm a boy."

"And a slob."

"I'm allowed to be."

"Because you're a dude."

"Yup!" He popped the "p," sending out a spray of crumbs.

"Gross," Val said, wrinkling her nose. Justin snickered. "And speaking of gross, are you and Ryan still doing that science project together?"

He nodded. "Yeah but we haven't started it yet. We're waiting for the mold to grow."

Val raised an eyebrow. "Mold?"

"Yup." He grinned up at her in a way that only a true kid could, one that knew he could gross out any human being if he was given the chance.

"Ugh, don't tell me," she moaned although she was secretly glad that her brother and Ryan were still friends, especially after the whole incident with Brandon. The last thing she wanted was to see her little brother suffer for something that had absolutely nothing to do with him.

It doesn't have anything to do with you either but yet you're suffering, a small voice sneered in the back of her brain.

She ignored it.

As her brother explained the use of mold in certain types of cheeses, Val welcomed the distraction and tried to keep a straight face. She nodded and *hmm*ed in all the right places, feeling a strange sense of pride at Justin's use of scientific terms that even though made no sense to her, seemed to make perfect sense to him.

"Moldy cheeses," she said when he paused to take a bite of his treat. "Sounds pretty tasty."

He grimaced. "It's gross."

"What're you doing your project on is gross."

"It's science."

"It's mold."

"Moldy science?"

"Or scientific mold?"

He laughed, flashing teeth caked in chocolate. Val found herself unable to resist joining in. It was almost a return to normalcy, for one brief moment and she breathed a little easier.

Until she saw the gold-colored SUV parked in front of their apartment building.

Her heart thudded to a halt at the same time her feet did. The world slowed around her. There were misfires going off in her brain, countless misfires until one connected with a painful jolt.

That SUV.

That dress.

It was the same car Sam had gotten into on the day she left the apartment wearing that tiny black dress that Brandon was so fond of. The same day she had returned home with that bruise. The same day Val had decided to find out just what the hell was going on.

It couldn't be a coincidence, she decided, not with the guy who leaned so casually against the car like he owned it and certainly not with the way he was looking right at Val as if he'd been waiting for her. She felt cold all of a sudden even though the late afternoon sun was blazing away.

It took her a moment to realize that Justin was calling her name and her attention snapped back to him. "Val? Val, what—"

The guy pushed away from the car, coming over to them with a smile that chilled her bones. "Hey. You're Justin, right?"

Justin looked up at him, surprise registering across his face. Panic tore through Val like a knife. The guy came closer, his steps unhurried but somehow making her feel like he was stalking them like a predator in the jungle. Justin frowned, taking a hesitant step back. The chocolate smears around his mouth made him look like some kind of demon that had been feasting on human body parts. Val's breath caught when she saw the guy's hand reach out to him. His hand dripped with corruption and disease, thick, black and gelatinous and it was imperative—absolutely without a shadow of a doubt—that it not go anywhere near her little brother. As if breaking free of some invisible hold, she shifted hard into protective mode.

"Justin!" she said, her voice loud and sharp.

Justin spun around, his confusion even more evident as she reached for him and took hold of his shoulder. She pushed him back, coming between him and that hand.

"Val, who's—"

"Hi. You must be Val." The guy smiled at her and the cold feeling that had come over her intensified.

She took a step back, taking Justin with her. She could feel him struggling behind her, trying to look around her. "Go inside, Justin," she said.

He tensed. "What—"

"Go on."

Pulling away from her grip almost reluctantly, he retreated up the steps. She felt more than heard him look back several times. She wasn't sure if it was curiosity or maybe he was experiencing the same bad feeling she was in the presence of this stranger and didn't want to leave her alone with him.

This stranger who knew them.

Without taking her eyes off of him, she waited until the door closed behind Justin. The guy's smile widened.

She braced herself as he drawled lazily, "Nice to finally meet you."

"Who are you?"

"Name's Edward but most people call me Ed."

"What are you doing here, Ed?"

"I'm a friend of your sister's. Do you know if she's home?"

Val's entire body felt like a coiled spring. He didn't look like any friend of Sam's or anybody else's, for that matter. His voice crunched and hissed like static, curling into her ears like painful electric fingers. The small hairs on the back of her neck stood up as she looked into his eyes. They were a strange gray color, like looming thunderclouds and they were dead-looking, like a shark's.

She remembered going to the Baltimore Aquarium and walking through the shark exhibit. It'd been poorly-lit and creepy—a lot like this Ed character who stood in front of her, almost posing with one hip cocked. His thumbs were hooked into his belt and the smile on his face felt like sandpaper across a paper cut. She supposed on another level, that he was handsome. High cheekbones, thick, plump lips, a hawk-like nose and a muscular build that he didn't bother hiding under a tight blue tank top, baggy jeans and an open button down shirt.

A blue visor was twisted backwards on his head, revealing thick, black hair that shone greasily with too much hair product. He was taller than Val but shorter than Sam and *dangerous*. It hummed off his skin like heat from the black top on a humid afternoon. It didn't matter how he smiled or how cute he looked when he did it; how he cocked his head almost playfully to one side as if Val had done something to amuse him. The threat that he exuded was barely contained. It made Val shift uneasily, feeling a little too much like a rabbit caught in the sights of a circling eagle.

'*He said we could do what we wanted.*'

Her heart already accelerating at a frightening clip nearly cracked through her rib cage.

He.

This dude was the he.

As if sensing her thoughts, his smile darkened, twisting into something like candy-coated cyanide. His dead eyes seared a leisurely path down her body, stopping at all the places that he knew would probably make her uncomfortable. She stayed unmoving beneath his scrutiny. Her mind screamed with nearly a dozen things to do; call the cops, scream, scream *at him*, kick him where it hurts, talk to him, reason with him, do something, but her body refused to act. She'd never even been in a fight before. Fights were Sam's department. It was the only reason she could come up with as to why she wasn't *doing anything*.

She felt like a fool. For all her talk about wanting to help Sam, she couldn't *even move*.

"So," Ed said when his eyes came back to her face. "Is she home?"

"I—I'm not sure. I just got here."

"Well, can you go in and check and if she's there, could you tell her to come out please?"

The request was so polite, so matter-of-fact, that Val had a moment to think *sure, why not* but then mentally reared back.

No.

No, she would not do this.

Maybe she didn't know how to handle fights. Maybe she didn't know the correct way to handle this situation, but there was no way she was going to make it easy for this guy to get to Sam. She had a feeling that he was used to people doing exactly what he said and she would be damned if she was going to be one of those people. One Delton was enough to have at his beck and call. The very thought of that made her bristle, made the sense of unease back away a little bit, replaced by that fiery streak of protection. She stood between him and their home and squared her shoulders.

"She's not allowed to come out."

He looked amused. "And why's that?"

"She's grounded."

"Is she?" he laughed and it sounded like nails on a chalkboard. "I was wondering why your dad was walking her home from school."

"You're watching her?"

"I always watch my merchandise."

Val's ears went red. She was so shocked by his blatant admission that she couldn't speak for a moment. "She is *not* merchandise," she spluttered with indignation.

He smirked at her. "You don't think so? I do. She's my best product."

"You're disgusting."

"Sweetheart, you don't know half of it."

"I don't care. I'm going to call the cops. What you're doing is illegal."

"Says who?"

"She's seventeen!"

"Not when she's working for me."

She couldn't believe what she was hearing. She just couldn't believe it. "Get away from here. Now," she demanded, her voice beginning to shake.

He took a step closer to her. "Not until I see Sam."

"No."

"Then I'm not going anywhere."

"I'll call the cops. I'm not kidding."

"And what are you going to tell them?"

She started to answer but he took another step towards her. Without thinking, she backed away which made his grin stretch wider, colder across his face. She felt the bottom step at her heels. Unable to move further away without letting him up the steps of her apartment building—because there was *no way* that was going to happen—she forced herself to endure the closing gap between them. His eyes were unwavering, pinned on her face like gray butterflies. It made her skin itch.

"I'll tell them exactly what's going on," she said, flushing when the shake in her voice became more pronounced.

"And you think you know what's going on?"

"Yes."

He laughed suddenly. It was low and mocking, full of icicles. "This is cute. It really is. Little sister looking out for big sister. Who would've thought?"

"Does it surprise you?"

"It does actually."

"Why?"

"You and Sam aren't exactly close."

God, what has Sam told this guy?

"So? Does that mean I'm not supposed to care when there's some creep like you trying to—"

He was suddenly in her face, moving so quickly it was like he'd materialized out of thin air. All traces of humor were gone from his face as if blown away by the wind. Her words lodged in her throat as she stared up at him. The thrum of danger was like bees skittering along her skin, poised to strike. She screamed at herself to run, to get away because sure, it was broad daylight and there were dozens of people around but she knew that most people didn't bother to help anyone in trouble, whether it was right in front of them or down the street. She'd seen it on TV a thousand times, saw it happen in school too. She herself was guilty of it but now it was a different story when she was the one in trouble.

"Careful, little girl, careful," he whispered. "You don't know who you're talking to."

His breath smelled like stale mint.

"Y—Yes, I do," she stammered. "And I'm not impressed."

He let out something that was close to a snarl and jerked his head forward, pressing his face into her jaw. Val gasped, bringing her hands up to push him away. His breath was hot and quick against her neck, his face warm and stubbly. "You—"

"Hey, hey, what the hell? Miss, are you okay? This guy bothering you?"

Ed jumped back away from her as if he'd been burned. They both turned to find a man standing next to them, frowning.

"Wh—What?" Val spluttered, her head spinning.

"You okay? You want me to call the cops?" the man demanded, looking reproachfully at Ed.

Ed put his hands up and flashed what in no way resembled an easy smile. "Hey, no, that's not necessary. Really, it's not. We're just talking."

"Well, it doesn't look like 'just talking' to me," the man said with a frown. "I think you'd better leave."

Ed's smile was sharp as he turned to look at Val. She blinked at him. He nodded, his eyes never leaving her face. "I think you're right, sir," he said. "I believe I'm finished here."

He beamed a smile at the Good Samaritan then sauntered to his car. He looked back over his shoulder, his eyes hard and empty, but the smile he flashed was mean and vicious. Val watched him go, her knees knocking together. Her breath shook out of her lips and she tried to focus when she realized that the man was talking to her.

"You all right, miss? I can walk you home if you like."

She swallowed twice before she found her voice. "What...oh, no, no, it's okay. I live right here."

"Did you know that guy?"

"Not...Not really."

The man shook his head in disapproval. "All the more reason for you to stay away from him." He started off down the street.

She stared after him then belatedly called out, "Thank you!"

He gave a small wave over his shoulder and continued on his way. She turned and caught sight of the tail lights of Ed's car as they disappeared around the corner. Her mouth filled with the bitter tang of blood and she realized she'd bitten the inside of her cheek.

"Val?"

Startled she spun around to see her father at the top of the steps. "Hey. Hey, Dad," she said, clearing her throat.

"You okay?" he asked, putting his hands on his hips and looking up and down the street.

"Yeah, yeah, I'm okay," she replied, straining to smile.

"You sure? Justin said there was a guy out here, looking pretty creepy."

Creepy. Yeah that's definitely one way of putting it.

"Oh, him. Yeah, just some guy from school."

"What did he want?"

Val looked up at him. There were bags under his eyes and he looked like he hadn't slept again last night. His haggard appearance made it easier for her to lie.

"He wanted my trig homework."

Her father blinked in surprise. "You serious? Did he tail you home or something?"

"Yeah. Can you believe it? Guy's a complete idiot."

"Sounds like it. Come on inside."

She followed him indoors, casting one more look down the street as the door closed behind her. She climbed the steps on shaky legs, trying to slow the adrenaline that was shooting through her.

Sam cornered her almost immediately, dragging her unceremoniously into her room.

"God, get off," Val snapped, yanking her arm out of Sam's tight grasp.

"What the hell is going on?" Sam hissed in her face. "Who were you talking to outside?"

Val met her eyes, saw the clear blue irises, so different from Ed's stormy gray ones. A wave of anger rolled over her. "Nobody—"

"Oh really? Justin came tearing in here, talking about some guy who—"

"It wasn't anybody, okay? Don't worry about it."

Sam's eyes flashed and she grabbed Val's arm again, crowding her back against the wall. "Stop playing the freaking hero, Val. Who were you talking to?"

Val tried unsuccessfully to get her arm out of Sam's grip. "You know who I was talking to. You probably knew he was outside, didn't you?"

Sam released her arm and folded her own over her chest. "Of course, I didn't."

"I don't believe you," Val said angrily. "God, Sam, what have you told him?"

"What're you talking about?"

"He knew Justin on sight. And he knew *my* name. Do you have any idea how not cool that is? Some random guy on the street, speaking to me like he *knows* me, who's calling *you* his merchandise?"

Sam's jaw flexed. "Val—"

"No," Val cut in, her throat threatening to close on her. "No, I...this is completely insane, you know that? You...this is all your fault."

There. She said it and it didn't get rid of the bitter taste in her mouth or the shakes in her bones.

"My fault? *My fault?* Geez, Val, are you serious?" Sam said, shocked speechless for a moment, which was a surprising feat.

"Yes, I am," Val pushed on. "You're saying it's dangerous. You're saying *that guy* is dangerous but yet he knows all about you, all about me, Justin and who knows what else you told him. You're digging yourself a hole and you're not even trying to get yourself out of it."

Sam threw her hands up. "What am I supposed to do?"

"You're supposed to call the cops, tell Mom and Dad, get some kind of help, do *something*. Not just let this idiot hover around, threatening you, your family, and treating you no better than a stray cat."

Sam's finger was inches from Val's eye. "I already told you. I'm freaking dead if I tell anyone. I will no longer exist if you, me or anyone tries to stop this. You know that, Val. I told you, for God's sake. You're lucky you got away from him without a scratch on you."

Val slapped her hand away, barely able to appreciate the look of surprise on Sam's face. "And what about the rest of us? What about me? Am I going to have to live in fear too because you're too stupid to ask for help?"

Sam's glare could've frozen the Atlantic. "It's not that simple."

"Yes, it is. You're just afraid."

"Oh yeah? Is that all?" she sneered. "You met him, didn't you? He wasn't exactly someone you'd want to go on a picnic with."

"He isn't exactly someone you'd want to hang out with at all. I can't believe you—"

"Don't," Sam said sharply. "Do not think for a second that you know *anything* about this."

"Why don't you just tell me?"

"Why? So you can throw it back in my face? Tell me that it's my fault? No thanks. You can take your self-righteousness and shove it up your ass."

Val blinked at her, realizing her mistake. She took a deep breath, trying to steady herself.

"Sam—"

"Get out of my room, Val." She turned away, shoulders stiff, her face an icy mask.

"I didn't mean—"

"Just go!" Sam exclaimed without turning around.

Val grit her teeth and surged forward, grabbing Sam's shoulder and tugging her around.

"Get off me!" Sam smacked her hand away.

But not before Val's fingers curled into the neckline of her shirt and pulled, stopping Sam from moving away. Something red and raw caught her eye.

"Val, get your freaking hands off—"

Gasping, Val pushed Sam's hands away, following her twisting body around until she got another good grip on the neckline of her shirt and pulled it down, revealing a long, *God, it had to be at least four inches*, cut that traveled nearly the whole length of her collarbone. It was thin, like a paper cut, an ugly, reddish-brown color, scabbed over with blood. The skin around it was painful-looking and bruised.

"Oh my God," Val breathed, staring at it.

Sam shoved her, finally dislodging her. Val stumbled back, nearly toppling over onto the bed.

"Sam, Sam, what the—"

"Get the hell out of my room, Valerie," Sam growled, clutching and pulling her shirt back into place. "I'm not going to tell you again."

"Sam, Jesus, that's—"

"*Get out!*"

The scream nearly burst Val's eardrums and she jumped. Sam was breathing hard, her face scarlet and she looked seconds away from clocking Val in the head. Slowly, Val straightened to her feet and edged around her sister, moving slowly, careful not to make any sudden movements as Sam tracked her progress. Guilt tightened her chest and the words at the tip of her tongue longed to come out. But the look on Sam's face locked them down.

She left the room, closing the door quietly behind her. Her shoulders rounded downwards, aching under the weight of this burden that she had made a whole lot worse.

CHAPTER 16

The weekend found Val at the mall. She hated the mall but it was either that or remain home, choking on the tension between her and Sam and trying to stop her screaming thoughts from making her want to puke her guts out. So when her mother, on a rare day off, announced that she was hitting the mall, Val jumped at the chance to go with her. She'd hit the book store, lose herself in some fantastic fictional story with unicorns, vampires, and elf lords because something false was what she needed right now. She didn't need real and she didn't need true. She needed something make-believe because the truth was too excruciating to swallow and the shame of what she'd said to Sam burned in of her chest like a flamethrower.

Sixteen years old and you want make-believe? the little voice in her head scoffed. *Sam's right. You do need to grow up.*

Val ignored it. She put on a cheery smile that hurt her jaw as she and her mother parted ways, promising to meet in the food court in an hour. She took the escalator down to the lower level of the mall and rushed into the book store as if hellhounds were nipping at her heels. The hushed quiet of the tall bookshelves and the sound of crinkling turning pages soothed her overtaxed brain. She breathed deeply, heading for the back of the store, where she knew there wouldn't be that many people.

Trailing her hands along the spines of the books, the raised letters of titles and author names glided smoothly beneath her fingertips. Even though the books were new, there was still that leathery, papery smell she associated with old books. The kind that always seemed like they were going to turn to dust in her hands if she turned the pages too quickly. The kind where the corners were folded, the pages no longer white but yellowed and the spine shot through with white lines from being bent by so many hands. She wandered slowly up one aisle and down another, letting her eyes glance over the books, not really reading the titles but looking anyway. She plucked one from the shelf and thumbed it open as she rounded into the next aisle.

And walked right into someone.

Gasping, she fell back a step, dropping the book. Hands gently gripped her arms, steadying her and she automatically began to apologize.

"Sorry, sorry, didn't see you...there..." her voice trailed off as she looked up.

"Hey," John said in a voice that was quiet as the hushed air around them. "Sorry. Didn't mean to sneak up on you."

Val blinked at him, long and hard. *I'm seeing things. I know I'm seeing things.*

John should not be in a book store. He should not be standing in front of her with his pale eyes smiling down at her, even if his mouth wasn't, and his hands as warm and careful as they were, wrapping around her arms like fur coats. Except that he was and she could feel the heat of his hands through the thin sleeves of her T-shirt. Her brain felt like it was short-circuiting.

Her mouth moved soundlessly, trying to emit some sort of noise but his cologne was clogging her senses. She was suddenly all too aware of how much she looked like she'd just rolled out of bed. Sneakers, track pants and a T-shirt as opposed to John's somehow meticulously baggy blue jeans, football jersey and ever present bandana around his forehead. She'd piled her hair into a messy bun on top of her head and *ewww*. He could probably see how oily it was because she didn't wash it last night.

Her brain finally caught up with that last thought and she felt her face burn. She took a step back as his hands fell away from her arms. She did *not* think about how cold her arms felt without his hands on them. Licking her lips nervously, she stammered out a shaky, "Hey."

He glanced down at the book at her feet. She followed his gaze then started to bend down but John got there first, squatting down gracefully on the balls of his feet and snatched up the book. For a split second, their faces were close—so, so close that Val could feel his breath on her face. She straightened quickly. John moved more slowly, gliding to his full height as if he were made of water. He held the book out to her.

"How's it going?" he asked.

Nonchalantly, she wiped her sweaty palms on her pants then took the book from him, careful to keep her fingers from brushing his lest her mind start sprouting ridiculous theories about electricity traveling through their touch. She cleared her throat. It felt as dry as the Sahara and sweat prickled along her scalp. "Fine, uh, good, I mean, you know," she stuttered. "How—How about you?"

He shrugged easily, sliding his hands back into his pockets. "All right."

She gave a jerky nod, tried to keep eye contact since they were talking and talking required eye contact. It was like rule number one of conversing with people—make eye contact.

Except she couldn't.

She took one look at his face and immediately, as if there were huge magnets on the floor, her eyes snapped downwards. She bit her lip, knowing his gaze was on her and unable to do anything about it. Looking around them, she started to fidget as the silence grew between them.

Come on, say something. What is wrong with you? Ask about the weather. Ask about school. Ask about any plans he might have for the weekend. You're in a book store. Ask him if he's looking for anything in particular. Just say something!

The thoughts screamed louder and louder in her head until she finally blurted out, "You never struck me as the book type."

She winced as soon as the words left her mouth. *You are so lame.*

But John simply shrugged. "I'm not. I was looking for you."

Val felt faint. If it was possible for this to get any weirder, the moment was definitely now. She stared up at him, too shocked to be embarrassed. "Me?" she squeaked.

The corners of his mouth flicked minutely upwards. "Yeah. I wanted to talk to you."

There was an ache in her fingers and she realized she was gripping her book so tightly her nails were ready to gauge right through the pages. Slowly she loosened her grip.

"How...How did you know where to find me?"

"Sam told me."

"I didn't tell Sam where I was going."

"She told me you were at the mall with your mom. I kind of guessed you'd be in the book store."

Was that an insult or a compliment?

"Lucky guess," she mumbled, shuffling her feet.

"Not really. I know how much you like to read."

Oh God, she thought as a rush of giddiness flowed through her. *This is not happening! There is no way this is real!*

She wondered what else he knew about her. The silly grin that threatened to take over her face pulled insistently at her mouth. "Yeah. I mean, yeah, I do. Makes me a kind of a dork, I know."

He cocked his head to one side. "I don't think so."

She met his eyes, feeling like she was floating. A part of her wanted to glance overhead to see if there were any red and pink hearts dancing above her head because, *oh God,* she was so far gone for this boy, it wasn't even funny. She didn't even want to think about the look on her face— probably something resembling a love-struck puppy dog but she couldn't *help* it. How could she when the leading man of her dreams was standing in front her, had deliberately sought her out and wanted to talk to her?

No one at school will be able to believe it. They'd gape and gawk and stare as she walked hand-in-hand with him down the hallway, as he wrapped those powerful arms around her, pulling her close, kissing her with those smooth, smooth lips. And then all those idiots who ever thought she was this poor pathetic loser who never went out on dates, who always stayed home on a Friday night to study, who never even *kissed* a guy, could all jump off a bridge because she was getting kissed by, in her eyes, the hottest dude in school.

She passed a hand over her hair, smoothing it against her head, biting at her lip. She started to smile like a loon as John said, "So I wanted to talk to you about—"

Oh my God, oh my God here it comes! Here it is! She held her breath, the "yes" ready to fly out of her lips.

"—your sister."

Ice water flooded her veins and the smile stuck on her face. Blood rushed through her ears and the crush of disappointment was staggering. "My...my...Sam? You want to..."

"Yeah," he nodded. "She been acting weird lately?"

Well, of course. You didn't actually think he was here to see you, did you?

Sort of, yeah.

Reality made a glaringly bright appearance and she flinched inwardly. She crashed back down to Earth, limbs flailing, landing in an ungraceful heap of her own stupidity. Geez, *of course* John wanted to talk to her about Sam. Sam was probably being as uncooperative with him as she was with Val, and here she was, entertaining lovey-dovey thoughts about a guy who was so far out of her league, he might as well be on another continent. He would never have a reason to seek her out, to want to talk to her just for the sake of talking. Why would he? And with everything going on with Sam, how could she even waste brain power on...whatever this thing with John was? A fantasy? A dream? Something that was never going to happen in a million years?

Well, you did come to the book store for a fantastic fictional story.

It was a reality check and a kick in the ass all rolled into one. This thing with her sister wasn't going to go away, no matter what book store she tried to hide in, no matter what little dream world she conjured up. It was going to be here, right in front of her, as real and true as John was, no matter what she did. She sucked in a deep breath, struggling for composure despite feeling so incredibly off balance.

God, you are such an idiot.

She needed to put some space between John and the barely-avoided accident of making a complete and utter fool out of herself. So she took a step back, an action which made John regard her strangely.

"You all right?"

She cleared her throat, shaking herself mentally like a wet dog. Then she finally raised her eyes to look at him. "Yeah, yeah, I'm good. What were you saying...about Sam?"

"I was just wondering if you've noticed how weird she's been acting lately."

Her sister's words echoed through her mind, loud and foreboding.

'If you get involved, I'm dead. We're both dead.'

She swallowed back a cold ball of dread. That threat would most likely extend to John if he found out. But wouldn't John be able to help? Wouldn't he be able to knock Ed into next week? Sure, Ed looked scary—looked like he could take care of himself in a fight. But so could John. Val had seen John in fights before and it was dirty, bloody and usually over within seconds with John coming out on top every time.

But who knew about this Ed character? Sam kept saying that he was dangerous. Val believed her but just how dangerous was he? Did he travel with a gang of people who were like him—cold, cruel and willing to sell their own mother to make money? Did he travel alone and if so, Val was sure he would protect himself by any means necessary. He probably wouldn't fight with his fists. He seemed more like the type who would bring a gun to a fight and then

John wouldn't stand a chance. She remembered Ed's empty eyes, his vicious smile. He would pull the trigger with that same look on his face, without batting an eye.

An image of that horrible cut across Sam's collarbone flashed through her mind and bile burned a path up the back of her throat. She turned away from John, trying to get her breath back.

No, no, she couldn't tell him. God, she couldn't tell anyone. Somehow she knew that the cut was punishment for her finding out what Sam was up to and if more people found out? What kind of injury would Sam be sporting then? Would she come home missing a body part? Would she have more bruises? Who knew what else lay beneath her clothes?

Her lungs jammed as she forced her gaze over the book titles once more. She hoped her nonchalance was authentic enough as she said, "She's my sister, John. When doesn't she act weird?"

"Yeah, but is she okay?"

"You talked to her before you came here. How'd she sound?"

"No, I mean, has she been weird in general?"

Val forced herself to move, her legs like jelly, going back the way she came. John followed close behind, his rumbling voice barely breaking the silence that enveloped them. "We're not exactly close," she commented. "In case you haven't noticed."

Maybe if we were closer, this whole mess could've been avoided.

Val sank her teeth into her bottom lip, her pulse pounding in her throat.

"I notice lots of things," he replied softly.

She almost tripped but caught herself at the last minute. She wanted very much to turn around, to see the look on his face that matched those words but she didn't dare. She kept her back to him, knowing he would see right through her if he looked her in the face.

He knew she was hiding something. She saw it on his face when he'd come between her and Brandon not so long ago. He'd stared at her as if trying to peel away the layers of her mind. She bit her lip harder until she tasted blood. The lid she was trying to keep on everything was already bulging, and to let it fly open would mean chaos. She didn't want to be around to find out how bad it would get. Clearing her throat twice before speaking, she replied, "Well then, I'm sure you've noticed that her being weird isn't exactly something out of the ordinary."

Silence followed her as she rounded into the next aisle. She could feel John's gaze searing into the back of her head. When she reached for a book on the shelf in front of her, she was appalled to see her fingers trembling.

"She can be weird but she's not that weird," John finally said.

"You might be surprised."

There was another long pause before he rumbled, "She doesn't come out with us anymore."

"She's grounded. You know that."

"Yeah, but I mean even before she got grounded. And trying to get her on the phone is impossible. If we weren't in the same classes, it would be like she disappeared off the face of the planet."

She'd probably be a lot safer if she was off the planet.

She looked at him over her shoulder. "So because you can't get her on the phone, that means she's acting weird? Come on, man, you know that being grounded means that phone privileges are limited too."

His stare was hard and unblinking. "She always finds a way, grounded or not."

Val's chest gave a hard lurch and she glanced away, leafing through the book in her hands. "Look, John, I honestly don't know. I don't know why you would think I have the answers. You might be better off just—"

"You know something."

The words were whispered directly into her ear, hot and *knowing*. She jerked around. John stood inches away, staring down at her. She licked her lips, squeezing the books in her hands. "What?"

"You know something. I know you do."

The bluntness and certainty of those words hit her like a well-aimed punch. Shaking her head, she moved back when he moved forward. "I don't know anything."

"Yes, you do. I saw you with Brandon."

"So? So what?"

He took another step towards her. "What's going on, Val?"

"Nothing! God, nothing is going on. What's your problem?"

Her voice had risen and it wouldn't be long before a salesclerk interrupted them. She tried to rein her emotions in but she could feel her control flagging under the steadily increasing pressure of his gaze, of his sheer force of will as he kept coming towards her.

He can't know, she thought feverishly. *He can't know what's going on. Sam will get hurt or worse, she'll be killed. That handprint will look like a paper cut. She'll get hurt before anyone can help her.*

Val trembled as Sam's voice reverberated through her head.

'*I'm freaking dead if I tell anyone. I will no longer exist if you, me, or anyone tries to stop this.*'

John came to a stop just outside of arm's reach. "Val, I'm not going to hurt you. I just want to know what's going on. Sam's my friend. You know that. You know I don't let anything happen to my friends."

Her voice sounded too loud, too forced. "Nothing's happening to her, John. She's fine. She—"

"Don't lie to me," he said carefully, a warning clear in his voice.

She felt the book shelf behind her. Fear pressed down on her from all sides. But was it because of him or the possibility that if he pressured her enough, she would tell him? She shook her head, a drop of cold sweat making its way down her back. "I'm not—I'm not lying," she gasped.

He stepped towards her again and his hand came out, fingers reaching for her. She cringed back, wanting nothing more than to get away from him.

"Val—"

The rest of what he was going to say was lost as she dropped the books and bolted from the store, nearly knocking over the frowning salesclerk who was coming towards them. She ran out into the mall, dodging through the crowds, adrenaline surging through her and she ran and ran, thought she could keep running forever if it meant getting away from this nightmare.

But she wasn't so lucky.

For the second time in half an hour, she barreled into someone, nearly sending them both to the floor. Hands steadied her. Breathing hard, she pulled away and mumbled a quick apology. "Sorry, sorry, I—"

"There you are."

Static filled her head.

Oh no. No, no, no, are you kidding me?

Slowly, like the next victim in a bad scary movie, she raised her head and the sight of Ed being so close to her, close enough so that she could see the clear outline of his pupils, sent shock rippling through her. His thunder gray eyes gleamed with a wicked light. She jerked herself back from him. His smile followed her, relentless and skin crawling.

"Good to see you again, sweetheart."

She gaped at him.

"Oh man, *this* is who you're looking for?" a female voice sneered from behind her.

Val turned. She recognized two of the three people in front of her from school. Greg was a tall, gangly kid who struck Val as the type who tried too hard to be cool. It showed in the way he dressed—the stylish clothes suitable on someone with more confidence—and in the way he followed people around, looking anxious and too eager to please, worried that someone was going to tell him to do something and he wouldn't be able to do it. His dirty, blonde hair was buzzed down to his scalp and his piggish nose and thin lips were too close together so that it seemed his wide brown eyes were lost in too much of his face. He looked nervous, his eyes darting around like he was expecting someone to jump him from behind.

Next to him was a petite blonde girl who Val had never seen before. She was pretty with bronzed skin and sneering, dark eyes that flicked up and down Val's body like she wasn't sure if Val was a bug that she should step on. Nonetheless, she flipped a shiny sheet of golden hair over one shoulder and walked over to Ed, sliding her arm around his waist and leaning into him. Her dark eyes challenged Val, as if Val even *wanted* to compete with someone who had bigger boobs, a narrower waist, and a preference for the company of scary guys who liked to own people instead of knickknacks.

Val looked away from her, her gaze landing on Jude. He stood a little away from everyone but he was obviously a part of the group by the discerning way he stared Val down. She knew Jude only through half-true rumors and glimpses within the crowded halls of school. His bleached blonde spiky hair was impossible to miss. So was his milk-white skin that left his eyes, as dark as night, sitting like two lumps of coal in his face. He had that chiseled look that was almost sickly-looking but always underestimated. She saw him once take a guy down who was twice his size after he made fun of Jude's name by singing—terribly off key too—Paul McCartney's "Hey Jude."

She felt something cold run up her back as she stared back at him. She didn't know him or Greg that well at all but she still felt like she had to worry more about Jude. There was something creepy about him; something just on the verge, like he was waiting for chaos to break out so he could join in. Although at the moment, dressed in loose-fitting jeans and a black T-shirt, he just looked bored and annoyed like he didn't want to be there. She supposed she couldn't blame him. She didn't want to be here either.

She tried to think past the jumble of thoughts in her head, tried to recall if she'd ever seen Greg or Jude hanging around with Ed before. Were they in on his little scam, too? Were they all business partners or something? Swallowing painfully around a dry throat, she said to Ed, "You— You've been looking for me?"

"Well, I think we got off on the wrong foot the last time we met. I've been hoping to rectify."

The blonde girl attached to his side reached up to nuzzle Ed's neck. He ignored her, his eyes locked on Val's.

"I'd rather not," she said.

"It's not a request."

There was mall security here. Rent-a-cops but still, it was security and if things got out of hand, they would be here within seconds to help her if she needed it. Yet, that thought didn't soothe her and she didn't think she could be so lucky to have a Good Samaritan help her out a second time. She suddenly wished she hadn't run away from John. She suddenly wished that she'd stayed home.

"What do you want?" she asked, looking from Ed to Greg to Jude and back again.

"Just what I said. I think you and I should start over. It seems counter-productive that you and I can't get along when your sister and I do."

Anger roiled through her and she heard the cold sound of laughter. She looked at Greg, who was smiling at her in a way that made her turn away in disgust. "Counter-productive in what way?" she demanded.

He lifted one shoulder in a lazy shrug. "Counter-productive to my offer."

She looked at him. He looked back, smirking and smug. When no explanation to this "offer" seemed forthcoming, she said, "You want me to guess?"

Jude made a strangled sound from next to her and it took a quick glance to see that he was trying not to laugh. Ed's smile faded into something more devious. Giving his blonde companion a shove away from him, he moved towards Val, his steps slow and measured. The girl gave him a dirty look and folded her arms over her impressive chest with an irritated huff. Ed stopped within arm's reach of Val, who was straining not to move back.

"It's amazing to me that no one's knocked out your teeth yet," he said in a low, dark voice.

"Who says no one's tried?"

"You need to watch that mouth of yours if you're going to be working for me."

Val pushed her tongue against the roof of her mouth. "I wasn't aware I needed a job."

"You want to earn your own money, don't you? Or do you like living off of Mommy and Daddy's food stamps?"

She glared at him. "My parents are not on food stamps."

"Even so, I think it's about time you were introduced into the workforce."

She licked her lips, vying for a courage that she didn't feel. "*You* think it's about time? What? Are you my father all of a sudden?"

A sick smile stretched across his face. "I'm going to be more than that when I get done with you."

Val tasted something nasty in the back of her throat. . How Sam had gotten lassoed in with this guy was completely beyond her. He was absolutely disgusting. Just talking to him made her want to take a hot shower.

With bleach.

And a steel brush.

"And what makes you think that I'd let you come anywhere near me?"

His smile got sicker if that were possible. "You don't really have a choice, sweetheart. You either work for me or I'll put your sister some place where you'll never find her. You wouldn't want that on your conscience, would you?"

His audacity was astonishing. Again she got the impression that he probably didn't hear the word *no* very often. She stared at him, trying to see if he was bluffing, realizing that she should've said *yes* when her father offered to teach her how to play poker. Would Ed really make good on his threats? Sam certainly believed he would. Val wasn't so sure. Lots of people made others do their bidding through fear. Tyrannical, psychopathic world leaders from centuries ago to the present probably had the same deposition and the same look in their eyes as Ed did at that moment.

She took a chance and squared her shoulders. "No. No, I wouldn't," she replied.

One corner of his mouth twitched. "I didn't think so and who knows, Valerie? You might even enjoy it. You can make your own hours and the payoff is definitely worth it."

"Does the payoff include getting beat up on a daily basis?"

Ed squinted his eyes at her. After a moment he said, "Only if you keep running your mouth."

"I think I'll give retail a try first."

As quickly as the day they first met, he moved and was suddenly in her face. She sucked in a sharp breath, craning her neck to look at him. "I seem to recall saying that this wasn't a choice."

Careful, she told herself. *Careful.*

"I don't think I'd be a good candidate for your job offer, Ed."

"Oh no?" he said quietly, his jaw muscles bulging. "I think you'd be great. You're the complete opposite of Sam; darkness to her light. And what better way to start a new job than to start it with someone you know?"

"Well—"

"We'll have to come up with a name for you two."

"I already have a name."

"I mean a working name. Something that really sets off your differences."

Val swallowed with some difficulty as his voice went lower and lower, his eyes gleaming with a strange light as he became lost in his own business promotions. Nausea rolled over her at what she could only imagine was going through his mind.

"Sure, sure," she volunteered. "A name. Right. Maybe something like 'Angel and Demon,' like that book—"

His face lit up like a kid on Christmas. "Exactly. See, now you're getting it. She could wear wings and you could wear the horns. Sweet girl-on-girl action is always—"

"You are one sick bastard."

The words came loose as if someone had plucked an orange from the bottom of the pile and an avalanche of fruit followed suit. He blinked down at her.

"Do you really think I would go for this? Do you really think I would let you treat me the way you treat Sam? What is wrong with you, man? Where's your brain, besides up your ass?"

His jaw flexed. "Val—"

"Do *not* call me Val. You don't know me. You think I'm like my sister? You think you can throw a couple of threats my way and I'm going to do as you say? Are you completely insane?"

She didn't know where the words were coming from, where this balls-of-steel bravery had been hiding. But it was there, hanging out and swinging in the breeze. She realized at that moment that she didn't care. She was not going to be coerced into the same horrible situation as Sam and if it meant getting her ass kicked in the mall on a Saturday afternoon while her mother waited for her in the food court, then so be it.

And when she got herself out of the hospital, where she was certain Ed was going to put her if the look on his face was anything to go by, she was going to find a way to bring him down. And if Sam had a working brain inside her cranium, she would help.

"You'd better say goodbye to Sam when you get home today, Valerie," Ed snarled. "Because it's going to be the last time you ever see her."

"No, it won't," she snapped back. "She's practically under house arrest. My father hasn't let her out of his sight in the last two weeks. There's no way she's going with you or anybody else, ever again."

Something inhuman and enraged came from Ed's throat as he all but launched himself at her. Barely having time to scream, she stumbled back.

A hand closed on the back of her shirt and yanked her away. Val tripped and sprawled to the floor. Gasping, she saw John come from out of nowhere, hurtling himself at Ed, landing a solid punch in the center of his face that had blood flying through the air in a red-beaded arch.

"John!" she exclaimed.

A shadow fell over her. She looked up to see the blonde girl glaring hatred at her. Instantly Val tried to stand up but the girl cocked a fist back and let it fly. Pain exploded through her jaw. She fell back to the floor, knocked breathless.

Wow, so this is what it feels like to get punched in the face.

The thought barely finished crossing her mind when a boot buried itself in her stomach. She gagged, curling up on her side. From above her, came rage filled obscenities and spit that rained down on her face.

"Bitch! Fucking bitch, fucking with my man." The girl was seething. "You and your fucking slut of a sister..."

Her diatribe faded away as she blasted her fist into Val's face again. Val cried out as her head snapped back. Scrambling, she struggled to push herself to her feet but her balance was shot as she was shoved and kicked back down to the floor like a dog.

"Stop it! Stop!" she tried to say, tried to get her hands up to push the girl away.

This crazy girl who she didn't even *know*!

But the girl came at her ferociously. She dodged and weaved, moving past Val's poor, breathless defenses and grabbed two tight fistfuls of her hair. Val howled in pain, deliriously wondering when mall security was going to show up. She cried out again as her head was wrenched forward then shoved back, connecting with the floor.

The world echoed, faded, then went dark.

CHAPTER 17

It was like waking up inside of a cotton ball. Everything was hazy and white and muffled. Slowly, she swam through the thick gauze of unconsciousness, poking holes, pulling cobwebs apart and opening her eyes. Groaning, Val slammed them shut as *bright, bright, oh my God, bright* pierced her eyeballs like needles.

"Valerie? Honey?"

She groggily recognized her mother's voice, thick with worry. She cracked an eye. It took a while for her mother's face to come into focus but when it did Val felt nothing but relief at the sight of something so familiar.

"Mom..." she tried to say but a series of hammers unleashed their havoc on the inside walls of her skull and she clenched her jaw shut.

"It's okay, honey, it's okay, we're here," Mom murmured, her hand cool and dry as she ghosted it over the top of Val's head.

"Wh—Where—?"

"You're at the hospital. You were..." Here she paused as if trying to collect herself. "You were unconscious, sweetie. We weren't sure if you had a concussion or—"

Val forced her eyelids to stay open, trying to hone in on what her mother was saying. "Wait, what—I was—"

"Jesus, Val, wake up and focus, will you?" Sam's face suddenly filled Val's field of vision. Her pretty face seemed torn between amusement and annoyance. *Yeah, like I got myself put in the freaking hospital on purpose.*

"Sam—"

"Yeah, it's me and you're lucky your head's already bashed in or I would've done it instead."

Val flinched as the sound of her sister's voice made her brain leak out of her ears.

"Sam, Jesus," her mother reprimanded before giving Sam a hard nudge away. "Valerie, honey, how do you feel? Do you remember anything?"

Val gave a long blink before trying to push herself up on her elbows.

"Hold it, hold it, lay back," Mom commanded gently but firmly. "Come on, don't move, okay?"

Following the motion of her mother's hands, Val lay back. Through watery eyes, she glanced around. She lay on a gurney in the hall of the hospital. The stomach-churning smell of cleaning chemicals, antiseptics, and stale bodily fluids was doing a number on her already-pounding head.

Justin stood across from her, at the opposite wall, watching her, his face pale, worried and angry. Val tried to speak to him, tried to assure him that she was fine but the words wouldn't come. Her face felt tight, wrong somehow and she reached a shaking hand to her head. She gasped in pain when her fingers touched the tender flesh along her jaw and near her right eye.

"Not as bad as it looks, Rocky," Sam said unhelpfully from beside her mother.

Her mother shot her a look. Val closed her eyes as the walls seemed to bleed around her. She cringed inwardly as she began to recollect her thankfully short lived time as a human punching bag. And God, then there was John...

Oh God, John.

With another pained groan, Val let her hand drop to her side. "Oh my God—"

"I hope you remember what happened," Sam said. "Because if you don't maybe the six o' clock news will help jog your memory."

Val gaped at her, horrified. "The six o' clock news? Are you kidding me? What—"

"The local news people were already at the mall covering some kind of charity event," her mother cut in. "The fight you were in, and I can't believe you were actually *in* a fight, Jesus Christ, Val. Anyway, the fight broke out as they began filming so..." Her voice trailed off and Val could hear the disappointment.

Val groaned. "Mom, it wasn't my fault. I swear it wasn't. I was just—"

"—an innocent bystander, I know," Mom finished for her, the concern melting away to a look of aggravation that was normally reserved for Sam.

To have it angled at her was something Val was not accustomed to. At all.

"Mom, you've got to believe me. There was this guy and—"

"Ed."

Val gaped at her. "You know?"

Her mother stared down at her, her jaw flexing in something that was close to anger but not quite.

"Sam's been giving your father and me quite a story, and it would be really nice to hear it confirmed by you."

Momentarily speechless, Val looked at Sam who was studying her fingernails a bit too hard.

"You told them?" she breathed, not sure if she should feel elated or not.

Sam shrugged then raised a haughty eyebrow. "So?"

"But I thought—"

"Valerie, look. It's bad enough Sam's been keeping this from us but you? I always thought that you were the more responsible one. And what happened today clearly proves me wrong."

"Hey, I—" Sam began, offended.

"Mom—" Val tried again to push herself up but a wave of dizziness held her down as effectively as if she were hogtied with cinderblocks.

"Just lay there and listen to me, okay?"

Val bit her lip, feeling like she was still asleep and dreaming.

"Sam told us about this Ed guy, about how he's been harassing her and about how he's been harassing you. My

God, the two of you! How could you not tell me or your father?"

Val avoided her mother's accusing look by looking at Sam, who fidgeted.

"I didn't think it was—" Sam said half-heartedly.

"What, that big of a deal? Of course it is! How could you think it's not? This guy tailing you home from school and you, Val, how could you not tell anyone he was actually right outside our front door?"

Val tried to get Sam to look at her but Sam was avoiding everyone's eyes now. But her jaw was tight, her brow furrowed as if she were having some kind of internal conversation with herself.

Val gave her mother a rueful look. "I—I thought, I didn't know what he'd do if—"

"Well now you know," her mother cut in. "Putting you and John in the damn hospital. Jesus."

"Is John okay? Where is he? Is he—?"

"He's out of it," Mom replied. "He has a concussion. He wasn't as lucky as you especially with it being two against one."

"Two? Wait, there were three guys there—"

"Yeah, but only two were fighting John, according to witnesses. Ed and his friends were already gone by the time the cops showed up."

The thumping in Val's head expanded to the backs of her eyes. "God, the cops?"

"Rent-a-cops aren't exactly skilled at breaking up brawls," Sam snorted.

"And the cops want to talk to you before we leave here," her mother chimed in.

"Oh my *God*," Val murmured in agony. "Please just knock me out again."

Sam snickered.

Mom shook her head. "None of this is funny. We all need to have a serious chat about the importance of a little thing called communication. I mean it. This is completely ridiculous and could've been avoided if either one of you actually had a working brain." She raked a hand through her hair. "I'm going to go find your father. Stay here. I'll be right back. Justin, come with me, will you?"

Val watched them walk away, their footsteps sounding like an elephant stampede. She took a deep breath then jumped when Sam threw an icepack onto her chest. With a murmured *thanks,* Val applied it carefully to her jaw, wincing. Her mind reeled and it wasn't just because she'd gotten her bell rung. She couldn't believe Sam had actually told their parents what was going on. It was nothing short of a miracle. She said a silent prayer, feeling the heavy weight released from around her shoulders.

"You're freaking crazy."

Val opened her eyes. She hadn't realized she'd closed them. Sam was leaning over her, watching her with a look on her face that was hard to comprehend.

"I—It wasn't my fault, Sam."

"Well, what the hell did you say to him that made him attack you?"

Val sighed tiredly. "Why does it matter? He's going to jail—"

"They can't even find him. And if he does end up in prison by some miracle, what do you think is going to happen when he gets out?"

"What're you talking about? After the things he did to you, what, you think any judge is going to go easy on him?"

Sam's silence was unnerving and the feeling of that heavy weight that had gloriously left her was now suspended above her head, locked in place, swinging dangerously.

"Sam," Val said carefully. "What? What is it?"

Sam pressed her lips together in a thin line. "I told them that he was stalking me."

"Yeah and?"

"And...nothing."

"What?"

Sam licked her lips, her mouth opening and closing several times before she finally got some words to come out. "I couldn't do it, Val."

Val stared up at her. Dread filled her. "Couldn't do what?"

She leaned closer, desperation written across her face, flashing through her eyes like lightning. It was scary that Val was now associating that look with what could only be increasingly bad news. As if this entire situation couldn't get any worse.

"I—I couldn't do it. I couldn't even say it. I couldn't say what he was doing to me. It was—it's—it's so embarrassing, so humiliating. Do you have any idea what would happen if this gets out?"

Val's eyes widened to the point where she thought they'd pop out of her head. "So you...they don't know—"

The heavy weight dropped on her, hitting her hard enough to knock her breathless. She looked away, pressing the ice harder than necessary against her face. She felt Sam's hair tickle her face, felt her torment and God, *the fear* that lashed from her like whips, burrowing deep inside of Val's flesh and hooking in, not letting her go.

"Val, come on," Sam whispered anxiously. "Look, the harassment, the stalking, that's good enough. We'll get a restraining order and—"

"A restraining order?" Val exclaimed.

"Shhh!" Sam hissed at her, looking back down the hallway.

"A restraining order? Seriously?" Val repeated in a lower tone but no less incredulous. "Come on, Sam, you and I both know how worthless those things are. We've seen enough of those lame *Lifetime* movies. A piece of paper doesn't mean anything and it won't stop him from coming after you or me or anybody else."

Sam's fist clenched into the blanket near Val's head, her face hard and trembling. "What do you want from me? I told Mom and Dad. I even told the cops. Isn't that what you wanted? Isn't that what you've been ramming down my throat for the past few weeks?"

"But you didn't tell them the worst of it," Val replied, her words coming out slower than she liked. "You didn't tell them—"

"Now you're splitting hairs," Sam said.

"I am not splitting hairs. He's using you and you're a minor and—"

"Val, if you don't keep your voice down—"

"I don't care—"

Sam grabbed her jaw hard in one hand. Val's words were lost in a shocked whimper as Sam pushed her head back against the gurney.

"Shut. Up." Sam's face hovered directly above hers, her ice-blue eyes wide, drilling into Val's head with a force that she could barely move against.

Pain ballooned across her jaw. Weakly, she grabbed at Sam's wrist, trying to pull her hand away. Sam's fingers bit deeper and Val felt tears leak from the corners of her eyes.

"Sam—" she managed but Sam's grip made it impossible to get a word out.

"Val," Sam said, taking a deep shuddery breath. "You really need to stop preaching. You need to stop talking like this is all so easy, so cut and dry, so black and white. It's not. Believe me, it's not. I told Mom and Dad. I told the cops. Ed was harassing me and that's it. That's all. They know about him and that's what you wanted. So leave it. There's nothing more that can be done. You won't have to worry about me doing anything with him or for him ever again, okay? Today cut all ties with him so that's it. All right?"

Val stared up at her and after a moment, Sam released her jaw but didn't move back.

"Sam," she croaked. "You have to get him on everything he's done to you. A simple harassment charge won't do a damn thing."

"Since when are you a lawyer? You don't know that."

"I know that because of those stupid movies you always make me watch."

"That's the movies, Val. They're not real life."

"No, but this is. Ed doesn't strike me as the type to obey a little piece of paper."

Anguish and frustration brimmed in Sam's eyes like tears and she let out a groan like a parent who was at her wits' end with an unruly child.

"I won't be able to go back to school, Val. I won't be able to face anyone if this gets out."

"But—"

"Jesus *Christ*, Val, do you have any idea what would happen if everyone finds out about what he made me do? About what he made any of us do? Yeah, sure, fine he might go to jail, if anyone can even prove any of it but the aftermath? What's left after it's all said and done?"

Val gave a small shake of her head. "I don't—"

"I'm talking about *me*. Can you imagine what'll happen at school? How much shit I'll get from people? God, it'll be hell, Val. You know the people we go to school with. They're like vultures, bloodsucking parasites. There won't be a single shred of me to salvage."

"Wait, are you—you're worried about what people are going to *say* about you?"

Sam flexed her jaw. "Wouldn't you be?"

"I—"

"Don't." Sam held up her hand.

"Sam, I think people will forgive you. You did what you had to do out of fear. God, none of this was voluntary on your part. It's not like you asked for this. You and everyone—wait, wait." She stopped, thinking for a moment. "Wait, you said, 'us.'"

"What?"

"Before. You said 'what he made any of *us* do.'"

Sam looked away. Val gripped her hand, bringing her gaze back around.

"Geez, Sam, there's more people? More girls like you caught up in this?"

Sam didn't answer for a long time and Val thought she wouldn't until she finally said quietly, "He's got girls in different towns. All afraid, all terrified, all threatened, all the time."

Val stared at her. The magnitude of the situation exploded into a realm that she couldn't even fathom. Her fingers tightened on Sam's hand.

"Sam. Sam, please, we have to say something. We have to stop him. We—"

"Oh, will you stop it?" Sam hissed angrily. "Stop acting like you can change anything because you can't. There is nothing you can do. No one will talk against him. No one and that includes me. Just—leave it as it stands now. Okay? Val, please?"

"Sam? Val?" Their father came up to them. His face was a hard mask as he leveled a stare of parental outrage at Val. "There's a detective who wants to speak to you."

Sam pulled her hand from Val's grasp and turned away.

Val stared after her, feeling small, helpless and at a loss. She had a strange sensation of standing at the helm of a runaway train and no force on Earth could stop it. She sagged helplessly against the gurney, barely aware of the detective who appeared at her side to take her statement.

CHAPTER 18

She was able to see John for a few minutes before leaving the hospital. He was still unconscious and looked strange without his bandana. His face was mottled and bruised, a horrible eggplant purple. His bottom lip was split and his one eye puffy and red, on its way to a nice shade of black. Guilt tightened Val's throat as she looked through the doorway at him.

Sam had given her a pointed look as if to say, *See? See what'll happen if you push this*? Wordlessly, Val had turned away to give her statement to a Detective Allen, who was patient and asked questions in a soft, consoling voice.

He seemed to know Ed pretty well, telling her in no uncertain terms that he and a few other officers have been trying to get him off the street for quite a while now. He wouldn't elaborate on what grounds, but Val had a feeling she already knew and the knowledge of that almost made her puke on his shoes. But she swallowed hard, backed up her sister's story then followed her parents out to the car.

"All they have to do is find that son-of-a-bitch," her father said as he climbed behind the wheel. "So in the meantime, we're supposed to, what, not leave the house?"

"They'll find him," her mother insisted in an exhausted tone that didn't sound all that confident.

"Sure, they'll find him as soon as they're done at the doughnut shop," he grumbled. He twisted around in his seat and glared at his kids with the exception of Justin who sat between Sam and Val like a statue. "And neither one of you will be leaving my sight anytime soon."

"We know, Dad," Sam grumbled into the window.

"No, no, not 'we know, Dad.' This is a 'sir, yes, sir' kind of conversation. You girls want to keep secrets? Well, tough shit. That will no longer be an issue in this family. From this moment on, everyone will know when you eat, when you sleep, when you're going to school, when you're coming home, when you're in the bathroom taking a dump—"

"Dad!" Val groaned in disgust.

"Oh, really," Mom rolled her eyes.

"I'm serious," he snapped. "No one's leaving the house by themselves. Adult supervision at all times. Period. Is there any part of this that is unclear to anyone?"

Val shifted in her seat, closing her eyes briefly against the too-loud volume of her father's voice echoing and re-echoing inside the car.

"Don't you think that's overdoing it just a little?" Sam asked after a moment.

His glare shut her up even before the last word was out of her mouth. "No. It's not overdoing it, Samantha. Not at all. So our little trips to and from school? Yeah, get used to them. If you're lucky, they'll stop by the time you graduate."

With one final glare, he started the car and they drove home in silence.

᠀᠀᠀

High school.

The lowest circle of hell made more prominent when you were the one in the hot seat. The place was positively buzzing with what happened at the mall. Val faced it with dread and frustration, especially since she couldn't talk her parents into letting her stay home for a few days, at least until the heat died down.

Prompt and solider-like, she and Sam were marched to school and deposited in front of their homerooms by their father, amid questions and taunts, stares and whispers, that never ceased as the day progressed with the consistency of gelatinous muck. Wanting nothing more than to hide in the bathroom, Val forced herself to go to class because even while sitting on the toilet in the end stall, she couldn't get away from it.

"Oh my God, did you see her face?" someone squealed, the laughter bouncing off the tiled walls.

"She looks *so* bad. I can't believe she's in school today. I wouldn't have even bothered coming in if I were her," another answered.

Yeah, you try telling that to my parents, Val thought bitterly, hunching on top of the toilet and bringing her feet up so that she was tucked into a small ball. She wrapped her arms around her knees and peeked out through the crack between the door and the wall of the stall. She could make out three blonde heads, each with the same pin-straight hairstyle and the same skinny-leg jeans. Val rolled her eyes.

"Do you guys know what happened?" one of them asked. Val could hear the *skriss* of a brush through hair and the snap of a compact mirror.

"I think she was screwing around with someone's boyfriend."

"I heard there were drugs involved."

With a silent groan, Val pressed her forehead to her knees.

"Drugs? I doubt it. Sam maybe but not Valerie. She's too much of a straight shooter."

Gee, thanks, she thought sardonically.

"Maybe not so much anymore. John's in the hospital with a concussion."

"No way!"

"Really?"

"Isn't he one of Sam's friends?"

"Yup and if he's involved, then you know it's definitely drugs."

Val gritted her teeth in frustration. The bruises on her face pulsed in sympathy or maybe it was mockery.

"Well, either way, it's hard to believe that Val's involved."

"What's hard to believe?"

"Dude, you *are* aware of who she's related to, right?"

"That's what I mean. Val never got into trouble before."

"You think maybe she and John have something going on?"

Val's face turned bright red.

"Ewww!"

"Gross!"

"No, I'm serious. They *were* together when all this crap went down. Maybe it's got something to do with that."

"That's too weird."

"Seriously."

"Hey, John's pretty hot, you know."

"Yeah, but Val's kind of a nerd."

"Kind of? More like is."

"What could she and John possibly have in common?

"Well, either way, if I were Sam, I'd be super pissed."

"Why?"

"Hello? Younger sister macking on one of her best friends *and* landing him in the hospital? Yeah, like I said. Super pissed."

"Macking?"

There was a slight pause followed by laughter.

"Okay, P. Diddy."

More laughter.

"So who else was there? Who was John fighting?"

"I heard Greg was there—"

"Loser," came a bored chorus.

"—and Jude."

"Jude? Ugh, that guy creeps me out."

"Dude, you get creeped out by your gym teacher."

"I do not!"

"Yes, you do!"

Their voices faded as the girls left the bathroom. The silence that followed was broken only by the hum of the pipes in the walls. Biting her lip to keep from screaming, Val stayed where she was. A fine trembling coursed through her limbs and she tightened her arms around her knees.

It was in that moment that she understood why Sam was so adamant about keeping the whole truth from getting out. With these dimwits they cohabited these halls with, there would be no way she or Sam would ever be able to survive the grinding session through the rumor mill. Just hearing the three girls speculating was a painful reminder of how unforgiving and cruel their peers could be, especially when they didn't have anything better to do than to drag someone through the mud. She didn't want to think about what else would be said within the sacred walls of the girls' bathroom.

Gradually, she found the courage to leave the bathroom. The bell had already rung so the hallways were blessedly empty. It was her lunch period and she made the automatic decision to spend it in the library. The lunch room would be a free-for-all and she was not in the mood for that, thank you very much. She slung her book bag over one shoulder. She was two steps from the library doors when a hand clamped down on her shoulder. Already jumpy, Val whirled around, knocking the hand away.

"Whoa, whoa, hey, easy there, tiger," Bryan laughed, dancing back a step.

"Damn, girl, you look like hell," Audrey snickered, her dark eyes twinkling.

Val rolled her eyes. "Thanks so much." She turned away from them.

"Hey now, come on," Bryan said cheerfully, slipping in front of her. "It doesn't look *that* bad."

"Hm. Well, maybe," Audrey said, peering at her closely. "I mean, I've seen worse."

"You've done worse," Bryan said fondly with a wink.

Audrey blew him a kiss.

"Guys, do you mind?" Val said impatiently.

"Not really," Bryan said, settling in and hooking his fingers into his belt loops.

He stared down at her, smiling. Val looked back at him, then at Audrey.

"Well? What do you want?"

"Bit of a smartass, I think," he said, the humor in his eyes hardening to something unfriendly.

"Don't see how," Audrey said with a raised eyebrow. "Since it was her mouth that landed John in the hospital."

Val turned to face her, blinking surprise. "What?"

"You heard me," she replied, with a hard look. "You got smart with some dude and now John's paying the price. Doesn't seem fair to me."

"Not at all," Bryan said, shaking his head.

Val took a step back from them, holding up a hand. "Now wait a second—"

"No, no there's no waiting," Audrey said, moving towards her. "You're going to tell us exactly what happened at the mall, Valerie or I'm going to give you another set of bruises that will match the ones you already have."

"Sam didn't tell you—"

"Sam wasn't there," Bryan said. "You were."

Val's gaze volleyed back and forth between them. "I don't—"

"Spill it. Now."

Bryan's gaze was relentless and Val didn't think that the simple fact that she was Sam's sister was going to save her from getting her ass reamed, yet again. John was their friend, one of their own and he'd been hurt. Because of her. Again, the tight feeling of guilt splashed through her veins and she swallowed hard against the lump in her throat.

"It—I—.Look, John just helped me out. He didn't have to but he did. I wasn't expecting him to either. He just jumped in from out of nowhere. . It just happened."

"Really."

"It wasn't my fault," Val insisted. "I didn't even start it. He came to my defense and—"

"What, out of the kindness of his heart? I'm having a hard time believing that," Audrey said with a humorless laugh.

"You two banging or something?" Bryan asked.

"No!" Val exclaimed, her cheeks flushing.

"So who was there?"

"It doesn't matter. It—"

"We'll find out one way or another, Valerie, so just tell us," Audrey said, with a bored roll of her eyes.

Val pressed her lips together in a tight line. "Okay, I— Greg was there—"

"Greg?" Bryan burst out laughing. "That loser? Are you serious? John could take him down with one swing."

"There was a girl I didn't know and...and Jude. Jude was there, too."

"Jude? Really?"

"Jude's a crazy asshole," Audrey said, sharing a look with Bryan.

"So John got his clock cleaned by Greg and Jude?" Bryan concluded.

"No, I mean, well, I'm not sure," Val stammered.

"You're not sure?" Bryan repeated sarcastically. "Were you too busy getting your own ass kicked to notice?"

Val clenched her jaw. "Something like that."

He grinned. "Let me know when you want some pointers, Val. I'll teach you some moves."

He feigned a right hook to Val's face. She flinched.

He laughed.

"So let me see if I understand this," Audrey said, trying to get the conversation back on track. "Greg and Jude were there but you're not sure if they were the ones fighting John?"

Val nodded even as an unwanted image of Ed floated through her mind. She certainly wasn't going to say anything about him. As much as she didn't like Audrey or Bryan, expanding this gigantic shit-storm to the two of them was out of the question. But Audrey stared her down just the same for a few moments as if she could sense what Val wasn't telling them.

Then Bryan said, "Well, looks like we'll have to have a chat with Greg."

"And Jude," Audrey added.

Yeah, I'd pay to see that, Val thought to herself.

"Anything else you want to tell us?" Audrey asked.

Val shook her head.

"You sure? Because if we find out you didn't tell us everything—"

"Val?"

All three of them turned at the sound of a new voice.

Allison stood in front of them.

Val nearly sagged with relief at the sight of her. "H— Hey," she said.

Allison looked at Audrey and Bryan. "Guys. How're you doing?"

Audrey sneered at her. "Feeling better, Allison? Walking a bit easier nowadays?"

Allison gave her a stiff smile. "Fine."

An unsettling silence fell over them until Bryan broke it by thumping Val hard on the back.

"Okay then, Val. We'll talk to you later, huh? Have a good day. Put some ice on those bruises, keeps the swelling down."

"Thanks, doctor," Val mumbled.

Audrey linked her arm through Bryan's and after shooting Val a dangerous look, took off down the hall with him. Val watched them go, ready to throw in the towel and make a break for home.

"Val? You okay?"

She turned to Allison. It seemed since forever that she'd seen or spoken to this girl and she recalled with a wince that their last conversation wasn't exactly...nice. She shifted uneasily.

"I'm—I'm fine. How are you?"

Allison shrugged, her blonde hair like snakes around her shoulders. She looked good—healthier with more color to her cheeks than the last time Val had seen her. She wore red and black plaid pants with a black T-shirt. A wallet chain hung low against her leg and her black combat boots were scruffy and familiar. Val felt tears prick her eyes.

"Good. I mean, well, you know, better," Allison replied hesitantly.

Val looked at her and bit her lip. She watched Allison's eyes move over her face, taking in the bruises. She waited for the inevitable but after a moment, all Allison said was, "You eat lunch yet?"

Val swallowed back a sob that rose in the back of her throat. "No," she managed to get out. "No, not yet. I thought I'd eat in the library."

"Be careful," Allison advised with a small smile. "You know Miss Cammin can smell a peanut butter and jelly sandwich from ten book shelves away."

Val laughed, surprised that she *could* in fact laugh. She ran a hand through her hair.

"I've got ham and cheese."

"Hm. That's probably around seven book shelves."

"Six might be pushing it."

Allison chuckled then chewed on the inside of her cheek for a bit. "Look, uh, do you...do you mind if I come with you?"

Val looked at her, suddenly not wanting to be alone. "No. No, not at all."

CHAPTER 19

The only thing weirder than talking to Allison was being faced with a little brother who, rather than going out of his way to annoy you, went out of his way to avoid you. And that was no small feat seeing as how Val shared a room with him. Tension was already at an all-time high in the apartment and things were definitely pretty bad if the "Little Buddha" was having problems looking his older sister in the face.

It was the first time since they moved that the entire family was home for dinner every night. Mom cut her hours back at the bakery, which Val didn't think was going to last very long once the bills came in at the end of the month. Their father was the designated babysitter, hounding Val and Sam every morning and every afternoon about schoolwork, gossip, who's-dating-who, and everything in between. At first, neither Val nor Sam had been very forthcoming. He had rectified that by tracking down their friends and asking *them* all of his questions. No one could *deny* him an answer. He was like a drill sergeant and you didn't talk back to a drill sergeant.

Completely mortified, Val and Sam then went out of their way to tell him as much as possible, to at least salvage what little dignity they had left. But dignity aside, it was an eye-opening experience to learn just how much their parents *didn't* know about their lives. Sam, of course, found it violating. Val just found it sad. It was so hard to move. It was even harder to breathe, and it all seemed precariously balanced on a thread about to snap.

After about a week of this special brand of torture and with Val's bruises finally beginning to fade, Justin approached her. He was stern and no-nonsense, standing next to the kitchen table silently until Val looked up from her homework.

He glared at her; his dark eyes way too serious for a kid his age. "You're an idiot," he announced.

Surprised, she blinked at him. "Thanks?"

"Don't make jokes," he scowled at her with a look that resembled their father's. "This isn't funny."

Val started to smile but stopped. She put down her pen. Letting out a long breath, she resigned herself to another ass-reaming, this time by someone who was too young to know anything. But as a member of her family, she figured he was entitled. She'd tried to keep him away from this mess, tried to keep him ignorant of Sam's stupidity, of the danger Ed posed, of her own carelessness of dealing with the situation but with no luck. It was difficult to say everything was fine when your face resembled a piece of bad fruit.

"Okay," she sighed. "Let me have it but be gentle."

He shook his head. "I just want to know why."

"Why what?"

"You know."

"Justin, I can't read your mind."

He gave a longsuffering sigh and sat down across from her. He looked at her for a minute then said, "Why didn't anyone ask for help?"

The question knocked her sideways. Even though she'd asked herself that a million times, it was mind blowing to hear it from someone who wasn't directly involved. Someone who was eleven years old; someone who obviously had more smarts than the rest of them.

She fumbled for an answer for a long time, finally gave up and leaned back in her chair. She met her brother's eyes and gave a helpless shrug. "I don't know. I really wish I did but I don't."

His jaw flexed and it was such a Delton move that had it been any other situation, Val would've laughed out loud and high-fived him. But it only made her feel worse. "That's not good enough.

"It's gonna have to be."

"No." He pressed a small fist against the table top. "No, I want to know why people are too stupid to ask for help when they need it."

"People in general or someone you know?"

"People in general but in particular, you and Sam."

Val pursed her lips. "That's a good question."

"Yeah, well, I'm hoping to get a good answer."

"Justin, if you want a good answer, one that'll actually make sense, you might want to take this line of questioning to Mom or Dad."

"I'm asking you."

"You shouldn't be asking me. I'm one of the stupid people, remember?"

"All the more reason to ask you."

Geez, when did he get so smart? Freaking Star Wars.

She sighed. "It's complicated."

"No, it's not. You needed help and you didn't ask for it. Sam needed help and she didn't ask for it either. Everyone always says that if there's trouble, you get help. It's pretty easy."

"Justin, it's complicated—"

"Then un-complicate it," he snapped, his round face set in earnest lines that were rapidly veering off in temper-tantrum territory.

A flare of irritation rose in Val's chest. She wondered if this was what Sam felt like when Val was in *her* face, preaching about the same exact thing. She looked across the table at her little brother, trying not to scoff at his ability to only see things in black and white. She forced herself to speak calmly, choosing her words carefully. "There's a lot going on here that you're way too—"

His eyes flashed. "Do *not* tell me I'm too young to know any of this. I'm a part of this family too and that means I have a right to know what's going on, age notwithstanding."

His last words threw her and she was speechless for a moment. Frowning, she twisted around in her seat, checking to see if their parents were lurking outside the room. When she didn't see them, she faced Justin once more. "Mom and Dad put you up to this?"

His top lip curled in a way that had *Sam* written all over it. "I'm not a kid."

"You're *eleven* and you're talking like a lawyer!"

He sat back in his seat, looking smug. "Nervous?"

"A little bit," she admitted.

His face softened. "People help each other all the time, Val. Total strangers help each other. They donate money. They donate clothes. They call hotlines and you won't even ask for help from the people you live with; *your family*. Isn't that what we're here for? Did you think no one would help you? Did you think you'd get turned down or something?"

"No, no, it was nothing like that," she murmured, dropping her gaze to the table. "I just—I was just afraid of what would happen."

"How could you be afraid?"

"Because of who was already involved," she exclaimed then winced at her raised voice. She took a deep breath. "Justin, do you remember that guy? The one who was waiting outside of our apartment building? The one who tried to shake your hand and I told you to get inside?"

"That guy?"

"Yes, that guy. He's dangerous. Somehow, some way, Sam's mixed up with him. I'm pretty sure she tried to leave him but he wouldn't let her. He made her stay by threatening her and threatening us, which is why she didn't turn to anybody for help. She was protecting us."

"Is this the same guy who hurt John?"

Val nodded

Justin frowned down at the table, chewing on his bottom lip. A sudden stillness came over him and he looked up at Val, his eyes wide. "Wait. Wait a minute. Ryan's brother."

"What about him?"

"Ryan's brother said something about a guy bringing Sam over to his house."

Val closed her eyes. *Oh God, oh no, he does not need to know this.*

She opened her eyes again and Justin's shone like black diamonds.

His chin quivered.

"Everything Ryan's brother said was true, wasn't it?"

She swallowed hard, leaning forward, her eyes burning into her brother's head. Cursing Brandon with the passion and heat of a thousand burning suns, she said as soothingly as she could, "Justin. I want you to listen to me. Sam did what she did because she was scared. She didn't have a choice. She had to do it or she was going to get hurt. She had to do it or *we* were going to get hurt. She did it to protect us, to protect herself. You need to understand, okay? It wasn't her fault. She was doing it out of fear.

Remember that time when we were at Six Flags and you wanted to go on that roller coaster?"

His brow furrowed. "Yeah," he said, confused.

"And remember how excited you were until the roller coaster climbed that first hill and how scared you became?"

Justin's face turned tomato-red and he looked away, grumbling, "I wasn't that scared."

"But there was no way to stop the roller coaster, was there? We couldn't shout for someone to turn it off or to back it up to let you out. You had to sit through the whole ride because you didn't have a choice. Remember?"

He was silent for a moment, weighing her words.

"That's the same kind of situation that Sam was in. She had to sit tight. She had to wait for the roller coaster to end because she didn't have any other option, Justin, okay? Do you understand what I'm saying? It doesn't matter what Brandon said. He's a moron and knowing him, he was probably making half of it up anyway."

Justin gave a half-nod of his head, still looking down at the table. All was quiet for a moment. The refrigerator kicked on, filling the silence between them. Val watched him, hoping, praying that her words were sinking in.

"So," he began quietly. "So if Sam was protecting us, who was protecting Sam?"

Words jammed to a halt, crashing into a confused jumble at the back of her throat. His look of disappointment said it all. Shame burned hot along the back of her neck. She balled her hands into fists, her vision blurring around the edges.

He pushed to his feet. "You ever try and build a house with playing cards?"

She had to clear her throat to speak. "Yeah, once or twice."

Avoiding her gaze, he picked at the edge of the table. "You know what happens when a card at the bottom falls over?"

Something thudded hard in her chest and whereas she always read about levels of metaphysical pain, she'd never actually experienced it until now. She hunched a little in her seat, watching her brother as if afraid of what he would say.

"The house falls down," she replied.

The sound of her strangled voice made him look at her. His eyes shone and his face was turning a pale pink as he tried not to cry. His mouth quivered.

"Yeah," he murmured. "Everything falls down."

CHAPTER 20

Torn between wanting to throw herself at her sister's feet or see how many times she could slam her head into the wall within a ten-second timeframe for being *so damn blind*, Val found herself standing in front of Sam's bedroom door. It was closed but she knew Sam was inside. She hardly ever ventured out, except to grab something to eat and to go to school. Val didn't blame her. It was probably the only place where she felt safe. She'd come out earlier when John called. He was finally home from the hospital and would return to school in a few days But after Sam hung up, she went right back into her room without a word to anyone.

John, Val thought to herself. *God, there's another one. I sure know how to piss people off.*

Multiple times, she thought of sending him flowers or a get-well card. Or maybe an "I'm-sorry-for-getting-your-head-kicked-in" card. But she didn't. He'd probably make her eat it.

She shook her head and looked at the door in front of her. She raised her hand to knock but her knuckles stopped centimeters from the wood as if a force had grabbed it.

Too late.

You're too late.

'*Who was protecting Sam?*'

Yeah, who was looking out for her while you were bitching about softball games and newspaper deadlines? Who was making sure she was all right while you were fighting with your only friend in the world and making googly eyes at a guy who would never return the favor?

The usually quiet but snide voice in the back of her head was screaming something fierce, loud enough to burst her eardrums. She flinched as if she were getting stuck with a cattle prod. She sucked in a deep breath and let her hand drop back to her side.

God, she'd been so blind. She'd been so adamant about keeping Sam at a distance. It was something she'd done for so long, she never even thought about it, just like she never thought in a million years that Sam would do anything to protect her and the rest of the family. Sam's attitude had always been selfish and arrogant. Their father said to her constantly, *"They have streets named after you— they're called one-ways."*

And now everything was uprooted and strewn about like garbage. Everything that Val knew about her sister was skewed and wrong, and in the time it took for her to notice, Sam was already in deep over her head.

In their deliberate quests to lead separate lives, how was Val to know what her sister was up to? They never needed each other for anything. They were so detached from one another, so different. Everything about them was so polar opposite that sometimes it felt like they did it on purpose so they wouldn't *have* to get along. Like it was more fun to be mean to one another than tolerant or nice. It was a lot like eating the last chocolate truffle in the box even though you knew that you'd probably throw up if you ate it because you were so full. But you just didn't want anyone else to have it.

Lately the thoughts of whether or not she and Sam had ever gotten along made her wrack her brain for something—a memory that they shared, a moment where they both laughed at the same thing, a time when they could be in the same room voluntarily and not cause some kind of argument. But she came up with nothing and she found herself almost making something up to appease the guilt that sat inside her chest like a giant rotten apple. They existed on different planes of reality. They worried about different things, cared about situations and people that the other couldn't or wouldn't.

It was like what Ed had said at the mall, *"Darkness and light."* Two things that wouldn't be what they were without each other.

Val remembered her sister's pleas in the hospital. '*Leave it alone*,' she'd begged. '*Please just leave it alone.*'

The turmoil inside Val's gut slowly but gradually began to thin and smooth out around the edges.

No, she decided. *I'm not going to leave this alone. No sir, no freaking way.*

Something was going to get done. This was going to
end and when it was over, there were going to be no more
secrets. There were going to be no more lies, no more
barriers, no more lines drawn in the sand that kept her and
Sam separated like rival warriors, no more obstacles that
kept them oblivious to what was going on. Val backed away
from her sister's door. She was halfway to her own
bedroom before reality sliced through the motivational
speech in her head.

She didn't have a clue where to begin.

❧❦❧

Her answer came in a form that she never expected.

For a few days, all seemed hopeless. She had thought
of everything from hiring private investigators to find Ed to
hiring assassins to take him out like Leon from *The
Professional.* But all of that cost money and connections and
what kind of money and connections did a girl her age
have?

Distracted, she floated through the hallways at school
like a ghost, ignoring the idiots who still had a few lame
jokes up their sleeve about her banged-up face. The bruises
were fading—thank you very much—turning into an ugly,
pea-green and yellow mottled mess. It was still tender to
the touch but at least she could smile now without wincing.

Allison tried repeatedly to get her to talk, but Val wasn't ready to trust her after everything that had happened between them. Allison seemed to sense this and backed off.

Not allowing anything to distract her, Val kept a discreet eye on Sam throughout the day, noting that she was almost back to her old self but not quite. As she strutted with Bryan and Audrey through the corridors, there seemed to be a tension set in her shoulders. Her eyes were tight and wary, constantly moving around like she expected someone, probably Ed, to come around the corner. Bryan and Audrey didn't call attention to it but Val could see that it bothered them. They also knew better than to push Sam for details. It made Val wonder if they'd ever had that chat with Greg or Jude.

Probably not. She would've heard if they had.

No sooner had the name *Jude* crossed her mind when the small hairs on the back of her neck were suddenly standing up. She glanced back, expecting to find someone in the hallway with her. But it was during third period and the hallway was empty. Frowning, she rounded the corner, trying to shake this abrupt weird feeling as she headed back to algebra class from the bathroom.

Man, you need to stop being so jumpy. Seriously if you—

The thought stalled out as she brought herself up short, inches away from Jude. The likelihood of running into him in a deserted school hallway was pretty slim, seeing as how the school held roughly over seven hundred kids. Unless of course, there was a reason for it, which would explain the icy grip of panic closing over her heart.

The incident at the mall was not far from her mind, and had it not happened, she would've concluded this little run-in with a "sorry-didn't-see-you-there" and gone on her way. But she wasn't that lucky. Her mind, having already crashed to a halt, was trying to gauge the distance between the two of them so that she could have enough time to spin around and run before Jude could reach out with one of those long white gangly arms of his and yank her back like an octopus.

Having never seen him this close up, Val's eyes moved over his face, hysterically deciding that while no, he wasn't bad looking, he was definitely someone to watch. As in *be-careful-where-you-put-your-purse* kind of a watch. His dark, dark eyes seemed to glow like banking embers, drilling into her head as if he were trying to see what the inside of her brain looked like. His jaw moved to one side as he stared back at her, giving her the same onceover that she was giving him. When his gaze finally came back to hers, she started to take a quick step back, finally ripping her feet loose from the paralyzing grip the floor had on them and listening to the desperate *run* that was being whispered into her ear.

He's with Ed! You need to get the hell out of here! Now!

Seeming to anticipate her move, Jude mirrored her movement, coming forward with one white, white hand outstretched and it wasn't until his fingers, strong and steely, closed around her upper arm, did she open her mouth to scream.

"Oh my God, don't even," Jude said with a roll of his eyes.

His other hand came up and clamped over her mouth.

Val's muffled protests were cut off and she jerked back, trying to tear free. His hand tightened around her arm and with a groan of impatience dragged her into a small alcove in the wall that most students used for make-out sessions. Knowing that Jude probably didn't have kissing in mind, Val fought harder, kicking and swinging at him with her free arm.

"Ow!" he snarled, shoving her away. "Will you calm down, please? I'm not going to hurt you."

"What're you doing?" she gasped. "What do you want?"

He rubbed at his shoulder that she'd connected with a fist. The look he gave her wasn't of anger or even cruel glee but more like exasperation. She pressed back into the wall, trying but failing to put more space between them.

"I want you to calm the hell down. Geez, not everyone wants to kick your ass, you know," he said with a bored sneer.

"Well, excuse me, but the last time we met proved otherwise."

He gave a sardonic smile, flashing even white teeth that seemed almost pointy. She glanced out into the hallway, hoping that someone, anyone would walk by.

"Last time we met?" Jude repeated, feigning innocence. "Oh yeah, last time we met, yeah, that went a little...unplanned."

"Yeah, and how exactly was it supposed to go?"

He gave a careless shrug. "With you being less of a smartass. Although it was pretty entertaining," he added.

She sucked in a deep breath through her nose. She caught a whiff of his cologne and it was surprisingly nice, manly. He moved closer to her until he was directly across from her, leaning casually against the opposite wall. He stared down at her, his look skeptical but somehow amused. It made Val uncertain and that annoyed her. There was nothing amusing about any of this and she seemed to be the only person who thought so.

Squaring her shoulders as best she could and trying to ignore the fact that the width of the alcove put her so close to him that she could feel every breath he exhaled against her face, she frowned at him. "Glad it wasn't a total waste," she said dryly.

He chuckled and there was real humor behind it. "Like I said. Smartass. That's what keeps getting you in trouble."

"It's not my fault your friends think they can do whatever they want."

"My friends?"

"Yeah."

"You know my friends?"

"Yeah."

He chuckled again and this time there was something sharper behind it. "No, you don't."

"I—"

"Valerie, you don't know anything about me."

He closed the distance between them. Her breath caught as he moved into her, crowding her back until her shoulder blades tried to dig holes through the wall. His hands came up to rest on the wall on either side of her head, bracketing her.

Trapping her.

Caught.

The word bounced unpleasantly through her head. It was suddenly hard to breathe. Panic tasted metallic in the back of her throat when she felt his face above hers, his nose feather-brushing along her temple. He was so close, his body warm and hard against hers and she felt more than heard him take a deep breath. He hummed it out in a way that was like he'd taken a bite of something truly delicious. Her face flushed.

Push him away, you moron! What're you doing? Get away from him!

But her limbs were paralyzed. Every fiber of her being seemed to hang on a fraying thread, waiting, wondering what he was going to do, which didn't make any *sense* because she didn't want to know. She wanted away from him, away from this alcove, God, away from her life. She squeezed her eyes shut. Sweat popped out along her hairline.

"G—Get away from me," she tried to say but it came out as a squeak, her tongue practically glued to the roof of her mouth.

When he spoke, his lips moved gently against her cheek, causing an outbreak of goosebumps to march along the back of her neck. His breath was warm and minty and she opened her eyes.

"You don't know anything about me, Valerie," he murmured softly. "But I suppose this is as good a time as any to change that, hmmm?"

A small cry broke from her lips as his leg slid between hers. His hips pressed hers and ice flowed through her body. She couldn't believe how she got here. She couldn't understand how she'd been walking back to class from the bathroom and was now pressed against a wall, unable to move as Jude did...oh God, as he did...God, what *was* he doing? A tremor went through her. She blinked rapidly as tears pressed against her eyes.

"No..."

"Shhh," he whispered, his voice almost soothing. "Shhh, it's okay. It's all right. Girls like this."

Not me! I don't! I don't like this!

She felt suffocated, frantic, her breathing so quick and so loud it filled the tiny alcove so that it seemed the walls themselves were taking in air. She tried to tell him to get away, to stop but the words choked her.

"Shhh," he cooed again when she shook her head.

His mouth moved back to her ear. "Touch me."

Her eyes slammed shut again like that alone could remove her from this nightmare.

"No..." she said hoarsely, too afraid to speak at anything above a whisper but then she gasped and that sound was deafening as his leg pressed harder between hers, forcing her knees apart.

"Jude...no..."

"Valerie. Put your hands on me. Now," he ordered.

No! No, no, no nonononono...

She couldn't stop shaking. God, she'd never been so terrified in her entire life.

"Valerie, it's not going to hurt. Come on. Just do as I say. Come on, just take it easy, okay?"

His voice was smug, amused like he had her right where he wanted her. For a moment, she thought of Sam and wondered if this is what she'd endured—this helplessness, this forced submission by a guy who didn't know how to take *no* for an answer, this fear that was all encompassing with no way out.

As Jude's mouth danced around her ear, she knew with certainty that this was a first glimpse into Sam's world. A beginner's taste of the things that Sam had done, had been forced to do and the aftermath of debasement and humiliation, the bruises, the cuts serving as constant reminders of what she'd chosen not of her own free will, but to protect those she loved. Frustration shattered through Val's despair and she put her hands on him and when they touched his ribs, she began to shove. He made a surprised sound but leaned harder into her, flattening her against the wall.

"Get off. Get off me," she said through gritted teeth.

She ducked her head as his mouth skirted along her jaw. A pure basic need of survival overwhelmed her. The desperate chant of *get away, get away* resounded in her head like a gong being struck again and again. Squirming fitfully now, she pushed at him harder, gasping and jerking when his lips branded her throat like a hot iron.

"Stop…Jude, stop it!"

Her cries grew louder, gaining momentum as she began to break free of the numbness that had locked her in place.

With a put-off grunt of annoyance, Jude lifted his head from her neck and wrapped a strong hand around it. His eyes burned as he looked down at her, so close that she could see the clear distinction of his irises and pupils.

"Shhh," he hissed in her face. "Valerie, shut up."

"No!" she cried out weakly, choking as his fingers tightened against her neck. "You—"

She stopped herself, suddenly aware of how they were standing and the placement of her leg between his. Latching onto it as the only means of escape, she shifted her weight, letting her hands clench into his shirt for leverage.

As if sensing the blow she was about to bestow upon him, he grabbed her upper arm with his other hand, hard enough to make her gasp. He gave her a rough shake and she raised her face to his as he growled, "You kick me in the balls and what I do in return to you will make what Ed's doing to your sister look like a picnic."

She froze. His dark eyes were heated and alive.

"Then let me go," she said, shakily.

He cocked his head to one side, looking at her as if trying to work out a math problem in his head. "Would it be too much to ask for you to at least act like you want to be here?"

She gave him an incredulous look. "Are you kidding me? You—"

"In about three minutes, that bell is going to ring and these hallways are going to be filled with people who will have no choice but to see you and me looking rather cozy right now."

She glanced out into the hallway and licked her lips nervously. "And you're okay with that?"

He shrugged then loosened his fingers from around her neck but didn't let go. His thumb began to absently stroke over her pulse, sending a weird, warm shiver down to her toes.

"I've been part of worse rumors," he said. "Besides, doing this serves my purpose."

Frowning, she said, "And what purpose is that?"

He leaned his face close to hers until his breath fluttered her eyelashes. "To talk to you without anyone being suspicious."

Her frown deepened. "If anyone sees us, won't they be suspicious anyway? It's not like you and I are friends."

"No," Jude replied, his smile turning devious. "But we could change that if you want to."

Her face burned. Her hands were still locked in his shirt and she pushed at him.

"No offense, but I don't think that's a good idea."

He chuckled. "Actually this was one of my better ideas. I've always wondered about you." He brought his face close to hers and inhaled. "You smell nice."

She flinched away from him. "Jude, stop..."

"The bell's going to ring soon. We need to look convincing."

"*For what?*" she demanded desperately, twitching when his lips touched her cheek once more.

"You mean, *for whom.*"

The cryptic meaning of his words shocked her more than the correct grammar did. She tried to move her head to look at him but he pushed his face into her hair.

"What—What're you talking about?" she stammered.

"When we're seen as we are now, locked in lustful bliss," here she felt him grin, "reports will go back to a certain person who's been tracking you and your sister." His words were a soft rumble in her hair.

She swallowed hard. "Ed."

He gave a small nod. His heart pounded against her chest, steady and strong.

"He's got eyes and ears all over this school but he needs someone to get close to you, to get your guard down. To soften you up."

"And that someone is you?"

He nodded again. His thumb continued its soft caress over her throat. She fidgeted when his other hand slid around her to rest on the small of her back. She tried to arch away from it which only pushed her into him. He made a sound of approval. She shook her head or tried to.

"Look," she said, struggling for a no-nonsense tone while trying to put some space between them. "This isn't making any sense. I—"

"Didn't I explain it clearly enough?"

"No, you didn't."

"What do you need to have clarified?"

The humor in his voice grated on her already frazzled nerves.

"Don't laugh at me. This isn't funny."

"It kind of is. You're adorable when you're trying to be tough. Kind of like an angry kitten."

"Let *go* of me."

"Nope. If I do, the plan won't work."

"To hell with your plan," she snapped. "Why are you even telling me this? You're a part of this. You're a part of Ed's sick little crew. Why are you—"

Her words were cut off as the hand that was on her back suddenly shot up to clench around the back of her neck. She sucked in a quick breath through gritted teeth as his fingers sank into some pressure points. His other arm curled around her waist, keeping her pressed to him. She squirmed but it was like trying to move a brick wall.

"Now see? There you go again," he whispered against her mouth, angling her face up to his. "There you go with these crazy assumptions. Assumptions get you into trouble, Valerie. You should try and get the facts first before you start making things up inside that pretty little head of yours."

Trying to turn her head away was futile as his grip tightened around her. "I am not making things up," she said, her voice strained by the angle of her head. "I saw you at the mall. I saw you with Ed. You put John in the hospital."

"No, I did not," Jude replied, his hand tightening on her neck. "You were too busy getting your ass kicked to notice."

"How can you expect me to believe you?"

"Because I'm trying to help you."

"How? By dragging me in here and—"

"Would you rather deal with Ed? He has much more entertaining ways of getting people to do what he wants," he said with a nasty smile.

She opened her mouth to reply but the bell rang.

She jumped. Jude's nasty smile turned smug, and he laughed as she tried to pull herself away from him.

"No, no, no, you're not going anywhere," he said in a sing-song voice.

He released her neck and wrapped her up in a bear hug. She flailed against him, twisting like a worm on a hook. She cried out hoarsely when she felt his hand dig into the back pocket of her jeans.

"That's for you," he said in her ear as he pulled his hand back.

She sucked in a deep breath, her head spinning as students filled the hallway outside. The noise was loud and echoed painfully in her ears. She nearly lost her footing when he swung her around so that his back was to the hallway. Recognizing the gesture, she forced herself to calm down. That was when she realized that there was something in her back pocket. She reached back for it but Jude caught her hand in his. His lips brushed her ear.

"Valerie, what I've done to you for the past ten minutes is something that Ed does to a lot of girls. The only difference is that he doesn't stop. What I've done is a kindness and you need to know that."

She trembled, her voice catching in her throat.

"I've watched him expand this little business of his for nearly two years. It's sick and it's twisted. And you'd be amazed by how many people he has working for him now. I've never met anyone who couldn't be bought, who couldn't be swayed or intimidated by him in some way or another. You are the first to fight and you need to be careful."

Val listened, feeling something like fear flow through her. Everything was becoming that much more real and bigger like a snowball avalanching down a mountainside.

"Ed wanted to come after you himself and use his particular brand of...charm. But I talked to him out of it. Told him it was too dangerous for him now that the cops were actively looking for him."

"Why...Why?" she stammered out as one of his hands stroked to her hip.

"Because you wouldn't have survived another encounter with him and because he needs to be stopped."

She licked her lips. "Why now? Why are you doing this now?"

"Like I said before, you're the first person to ever stand up to him. And while it's beyond stupid on so many levels, it's also a sign for the beginning of the end. I've seen too many people hurt by him, and I haven't gotten a decent night's sleep in a long time."

She turned her face into his, making him look at her. His eyes were bright, like shiny black beads and there was something unreadable floating in their depths. His mouth was a scant inch from hers. The noise from the hallway faded to a low fuzzy pitch.

"But if he's your friend..."

He nodded and his throat convulsed when he swallowed, his eyes on her lips. "He is. That's why this needs to end. You're not the only one on the brink of losing someone you care about."

Val could barely breathe as she looked up at him. His eyes shifted back and forth between her eyes and her mouth. Then he was gone, slipping out of the alcove and disappearing into the throng of students. She caught herself against the wall, shaking hard and feeling in her back pocket for the small book Jude had put there.

It was a dream. It had to be a dream but she wasn't waking up and she wasn't sure she wanted to.

CHAPTER 21

By seventh period, Kenny was in her face demanding details about the make-out session between her and Jude.

"Valerie, Valerie, my good pal, Val!" he exclaimed, clapping his hands. "Surely if there's anything you want to get off your chest, I'm the man to talk to."

She rolled her eyes, dodging around him as he bounced in and out of her way. "You sure are," she mumbled.

His blue eyes twinkled. "Oh, come on, don't be shy! It's not like you're the first person to ever get caught playing tonsil hockey. Granted you were probably the last person anyone expected," he added with a grin.

With Jude hung unspoken in the air.

She felt the blood rush to her face. Her nerves had yet to recover from being reduced to a jittery mess after Jude left her in that alcove. Her mind had been spinning nonstop and with the way Kenny danced around her, she wouldn't be surprised if she threw up on him.

"I didn't get caught," she said with another roll of her eyes.

"No? Then what do you call it?"

"Nothing. We were just talking."

"With your arms around each other? That must've been some conversation."

The red in her cheeks deepened. "It's none of your business, Kenny."

"You're supposed to say 'no comment'."

"That will only make me sound guilty."

"True," he agreed with a nod. "And what better way to alleviate some of that guilt by talking to me?" He waggled his eyebrows at her.

"Sorry, got class," she called over her shoulder as she brushed past him.

Kenny faked an evil laugh. "You haven't heard the last of me!"

She ducked into history class, painfully aware of the whispers that followed her like yipping dogs. As she took her seat, conversations around her ground to a halt then started up again after a moment, speculating and analyzing as if they were all news people on CNN.

Val buried her face in her textbooks, pretending to be absorbed in wars from long ago, but she could barely comprehend the words on the pages. She kept seeing the dark depths of Jude's eyes and the dizzying, conflicting emotions that went from smug and arrogant to pained and defeated so rapidly, it was hard to keep up. The small book he gave her burned ferociously in her back pocket, and it had taken all of her willpower not to close herself up in the nearest bathroom stall and read what lay inside. Jude's warning of Ed's spies rung loud and clear in her ears and although she found herself believing that much, she was still reluctant to fully trust his motives.

It was true—he had given her something that was invaluable; information against Ed that no one else was willing to give her. But what was the price that she would have to pay in return? She couldn't believe that he would simply help her out of the kindness of his heart. Ed was his friend and Jude was sacrificing that friendship for what? What was in it for him? Was it really for the sake of others? Or was there something else that Jude was invested in?

'You're not the only one on the brink of losing someone.'

The pain she'd seen in his eyes was deep and introduced yet another piece of the puzzle that was ballooning outwards at an unstoppable rate.

Val sighed to herself and glanced at the clock. She needed this day to end and end now. She rummaged for some aspirin in her book bag, feeling the tendrils of a headache snake its way into the front of her head.

Finally, finally the last bell of the day rang and she launched herself to her locker. Ignoring the shoulder-checks that were too hard and too many to count to be accidental, she made her way outside. She spotted Sam and their father already waiting.

"Val! Hey Val, wait up!" Groaning under her breath, she turned and saw Allison making her way through the crowd. "Hey," she greeted her with a forced smile.

Allison gave her a concerned look. "Hey, are you okay? I was hearing some craziness today about you and Jude and—"

"It was nothing," Val interrupted her, waving a hand. "Really. You know how people get things ass-backwards around here."

"So you didn't—"

"Look, Allison, I've got to go, okay? Dad's waiting."

"But are you all right?"

"Yeah, I'm fine."

"Well, can I walk home with you guys?"

Val swallowed back her aggravation. Geez, all she wanted to do was get the hell home. "Nah, you better not. Dad's still on prison watch."

Allison bit her lip and Val knew she was trying to stall her. Her friend wanted to know what had happened. Like everybody else, the gossip was too good to pass up even when it was about a friend.

Val started to walk backwards, away from her. "I'll see you later, Allison."

"Well, wait, can I call you—"

"Yeah, call me later. Bye!" She walked away, her smile falling away immediately as if gravity was suddenly too strong. She could feel Allison's disappointment even with the growing distance between them but Val had bigger things to worry about.

Like the way Sam was practically *thrumming* with tension, staring at her so hard, Val was sure she would sprain something.

Her father greeted her with a smile. "Hey, Val."

"Hey, Dad. Sam."

Sam gave her a long look. Her eyes gleamed in a way that set Val's guard up. "Hey, Val."

Her tone didn't bode well either.

"So what's up?" Dad asked as they walked home.

Sam shot Val another look. Val's heart leapt into her throat. She began to shake her head desperately but Sam was already talking.

"Val was caught making out with some dude in the hallway during third period."

"Sam!" Val shrieked.

"*What!*" Dad shrieked just as loud.

"Turns out it was Jude," Sam went on with a cold sneer.

Her father's mouth was open in shock. "Jude? Wasn't he one of the guys who put John in the hospital?"

"Yes," Sam snapped.

"No!" Val shot back then cleared her throat when two sets of angry eyes pinned her. "Well, I'm mean, he said—he said he didn't."

"Oh, that's so comforting," Dad said angrily. "Since when do you associate yourself with people who beat up your friends?"

"John's not her friend. He's my friend," Sam corrected. "And I think I'd like to know the answer to that, too."

"It wasn't like that," Val said, taking a step back from them. "Guys, just listen to me—"

"Let's go. We're going to sort this out when we get home," he cut in sharply. "I'm not having an argument in the middle of the goddamn street."

He stalked off, leaving Sam and Val to glare at each other.

"You're a backstabber," Sam hissed at her. "What the hell is wrong with you?"

"I am not a back stabber and why do you even believe any of that crap? You know how things get twisted up when they're flying around school!"

"Girls!" Dad shouted from further up the sidewalk. "Now!"

Sam shoved a finger in her face. "If John, Bryan, or Audrey decides to kick your ass for this, I'm not going to stop them."

She stalked off before Val could respond.

CHAPTER 22

Much to Val's relief, the argument didn't continue once they got home but that was only because Detective Allen was waiting for them outside their apartment building. She remembered him from that day at the hospital, only because he was the only one who'd spoken to her like the whole incident *wasn't* her fault. He was calm and patient, gently prying answers out of her without her feeling like she was some kind of trapped animal. It was weird seeing him without her head pounding like it'd been trampled on by elephants. And when he shook her hand in greeting, it was almost like she was meeting him for the first time.

He was tall, taller than her father, middle aged with a full head of black and white hair. He didn't have the world-weary look that Val thought most police officers had. Instead there was a look of determination, of stony resolve that she equated with what she hoped would be good news.

"Mr. Delton, Samantha, Valerie, how are you?" he said with a polite smile.

Sam shrugged, hanging back with her arms folded over her chest. Val tried to smile.

"You look better than the last time I saw you, Valerie," he observed.

Val blushed and shrugged, looking down at the ground.

"How are you, Detective? You want to come inside?" her father said after he shook his hand.

"If you don't mind."

Once they were in the kitchen, Detective Allen declined an offer of coffee and took a seat at the table. Dad sat across from him while Val and Sam hovered in the doorway.

"Is your wife home, Mr. Delton?" the detective asked.

"No, but I can call her."

"That's a good idea."

No sooner had his words left his mouth then the front door banged open and there came a sharp, "Why is there a police car parked outside our building?" A half second later, Val's mother charged into the kitchen. "Someone better start talking...oh, hi Detective Allen. How are you?"

"I'm fine, ma'am. There's no need to—"

"Is everything all right? Why are you here?" she interrupted in a just-beginning-to-panic voice as she looked around. "What's wrong? Did something happen?"

"There's nothing wrong, ma'am," Detective Allen said, his soothing voice only serving to aggravate her further.

"Then why are you *here*?" she exclaimed, her eyes wide.

"Dear, have a seat. Please." Her father came up behind her and guided her gently but firmly into a chair at the table.

Dad took a seat next to her and grasped her hand in his. Then they looked at Detective Allen.

"Okay," Dad said with a deep breath. "What's the latest?"

"There's been a sighting," he began.

"UFOs?" Sam quipped.

No one laughed and she fell silent with a pout.

"There's been a sighting," the detective began again. "Ed was seen last night on the street where his mother lives."

Mom let out a long exhale of breath that ended with something that was almost a whimper. She pressed her hand to her head.

Val's father squared his shoulders. "And?"

"He vanished when we were notified but I suspect he's still in town. I wanted to come by and let you guys know that, and to also tell you that you need to be extra careful."

The last was directed at Val and Sam, who fidgeted nervously.

"What're we suppose to do?" Mom asked wearily.

"Keep doing what you're doing," Detective Allen advised. "But just pay more attention to your surroundings. Go out only if you have to but don't go out alone. Make sure there's always someone with you."

Dad nodded. "I've been walking the girls to and from school every day."

"That's good. Don't stop doing that until we catch him."

"Hey, cool, is that a real gun?"

Everyone turned to find Justin in the doorway, his dark eyes bright with curiosity as he stared at the cop sitting at his kitchen table.

Val's mother shot to her feet.

"Come on, Justin, let's go to your room."

"Aw, Mom."

"Now."

An unsettling silence fell over the room. Val cleared her throat and asked, "Can I, um, can I ask you how you found out he was at his mother's?"

Detective Allen met her eyes. "Someone called it in."

Val felt her heart skip a beat. "Do you know who it was?"

His eyes held hers. Out of the corner of her eye, she could feel Sam watching her.

"It was anonymous," Detective Allen replied, giving her a hard look.

'*You're not the only one on the brink of losing someone.*'

Val licked her lips and came up to the table. Her hands shook as she took out the notebook from her back pocket. She heard Sam choke behind her.

"I think I should give you this," Val said.

Detective Allen went very still. He looked at the book in Val's hand then peered up into her face.

"What is it?"

"Val..."She looked over at her shoulder. Sam was pale, on the verge of puking. She took an unsteady step forward.

Alarmed, Dad went to her side.

"Sam? Sam, you all right?"

Sam didn't answer. She kept staring at the book in Val's hand. Dad looked at his youngest daughter.

"Val, what is that?"

Feeling as though fingers were crushing her throat, she could only shake her head. She turned back to Detective Allen who was now on his feet.

"Where did you get it?" he asked quietly.

"Please," Val begged. "Please just take it. I think it'll be a big help."

"You didn't look at it?"

"No."

"You didn't open it at all?"

"No."

Gingerly, he picked it up by one corner and shook out a clear plastic bag from his pocket. He slid the book inside and sealed the bag. Val wiped her hands on her jeans and moved away from him.

"I'll be in touch if we hear anything more," Detective Allen said. "In the meantime, you guys be careful, all right? Call me if there's anything, *anything* going on. Got it?"

"But what is that?" Dad said, curling his arm around Sam's shoulders.

"This is something that will put Ed away for a long, long time," he said, looking at each one of them in turn.

"Remember what I said. Be careful and call me if you see or hear anything. Got it?"

There were nods all around.

The second the front door closed behind Detective Allen, Dad whirled around to his youngest daughter.

"Val? Start talking," he said with a warning in his voice. "What the hell is going on? What did I tell you girls before? Communication. Communication is *key* if we're going to get through this. You remember that, right? You remember me saying that?"

Val nodded, swallowing hard. Sam's head gave a twitch.

"Now what was that book?"

Val chewed on the inside of her cheek. "Jude gave me that earlier today."

"The same guy you were making out with?" Dad asked incredulously.

"Yes, but we weren't kissing. We were talking and he gave me that book."

"Why?" Sam managed to get out. "Why would he give that to you?"

Val looked at her. It was strange. She expected Sam to move away from her father but instead she leaned into him. His arm tightened around her shoulders, keeping her close. Val felt her chest loosen a little.

"To help us."

Dad shook his head in disbelief. "But—But John—I mean, why—"

"Jude said he didn't touch him."

Her father frowned, not satisfied. He looked at Sam.

"Come on, sweetie. You need to lie down."

Without resisting, she let him lead her out of the room. Val sank into a kitchen chair, hoping, praying she was doing the right thing.

CHAPTER 23

"Mom, we're not supposed to go out by ourselves," Val said for what felt like the one-hundredth time that Saturday.

"I think I can manage a few hundred feet to the bakery," her mother griped as she grabbed her purse.

"That's not the point."

"Will you stop acting like the parent around here, Valerie? That's supposed to be my job."

"Dad! Will you get in here and help me?"

"Hang on a sec!"

"You can always run to the bakery," Justin said helpfully, his face buried in a comic book. "You know, jump down the steps and let 'er rip."

"Have you ever seen me run, Justin?" Mom said. "I run like a penguin."

Justin snorted. "Happy feet."

The doorbell rang.

"Mom, will you wait—"

"Val, if you're going to walk me to the bakery, then someone else has to come along too so you won't be walking back here by yourself."

"Dad can come with—"

"Your father has to take Sam to the eye doctor, and I was supposed to be at work fifteen minutes ago."

"But—"

Mom swung the front door open. "John!" she exclaimed before engulfing him in a huge hug.

Val took an unconscious step back.

"Hey, Mrs. D.," he grumbled, laughing silently as he returned her hug a little awkwardly.

His eyes flicked to Val's over her mother's shoulder. She froze. Something passed within their depths that made her uneasy, and she took another step back as Mom let go of him. Mom gently touched John's chin, inspecting his face.

"You look good. How's everything feeling?"

"Better, thanks."

"Well, come on in." She shut the door after him.

"Hey, champ," he said to Justin, ignoring Val completely.

"Hey, Rocky," Justin said with a grin.

John chuckled. "Is Sam around?"

"Actually she and her father are going out in a bit and I'm so late for work." She started to edge towards the door but Val stopped her.

"Mom, I'm coming with you."

"No, you're not."

"Why?"

"Because then you'll be walking back by yourself and I don't need that on my conscious, thank you very much."

"I'll walk her back," John volunteered.

Val's blood stopped in her veins. She stared wide eyed at her mother who flashed him a big relieved smile.

"John, you are a saint. Let's go, Val."

She backpedaled. "Uh, well, look—"

"Come on, I'm late enough as it is. Bye, everyone!"

"Mom—"

"Bye, Mom!" Justin called out.

"See you later, hon," Dad yelled from the kitchen.

"Come on, Val. Your mom's running late," John said in a soft voice.

But Val could detect an edge of steel under that quiet tone. She suddenly heard Darth Vader music in her head.

She forced herself to look up at him. Except for some light bruising around one eye and a dark red scab at his bottom lip, he looked as he always did. A white bandana was wrapped around his forehead, setting off his bronze skin and making it even more impossible to avoid his pale green eyes. Baggy jeans and a white button down shirt with the sleeves rolled up normally would've made her swoon like a girl confronted with Robert Pattinson. But she could only remember what he looked like in the hospital, bruised, battered and unconscious. She felt guilt rip through her.

The look he gave her stopped the words on her tongue. The threat of tears loomed, and it was a feeling that seemed so constant now that if she ever *didn't* feel like crying, she would think that something was wrong. Silently, she followed her mother out, barely able to keep her balance on watery legs.

It was the most uncomfortable and longest walk to the bakery *ever*. Her mother talked nonstop, unaware of Val lagging behind with her hands in her pockets and her shoulders hunched like she was anticipating a smack in the head.

John kept his attention on her mother, smiling softly and nodding in all the right places. Val knew that Mom had a soft spot for him, always associated him with words like "grounded" and "good head on his shoulders" and "strong" and "intelligent" and Val's favorite, "sound of mind and body." She was pretty sure her mother would adopt him if she could but John's parents would probably have something to say about that.

The bakery was packed and smelled gloriously of bread and coffee. They fought their way inside to the counter.

"Don't go anywhere, guys," Mom said quickly. "I'll bring something out for you."

"No, Mrs. D., don't, it's all right," John said.

"Mom, it's cool. I've got to get back—"

"Hey, it's the least I can do for my escorts." She disappeared behind the counter.

At a loss, Val stared desperately after her for a moment before dropping her gaze to the floor. She felt John next to her, a big looming presence, silently watching people eat, laugh and buy muffins, scones and bread loaves. She snuck a peek at him, watching the strong line of his jaw clench and unclench as he chewed absently on a piece of gum. Her legs jittered and she balled her hands into fists in her pockets.

Come on, Mom, hurry up so I can get out of here, please!

John suddenly turned and looked at her. She shifted her face away so quickly she was surprised she didn't give herself whiplash and glanced out the window, concentrating too hard on the people walking by outside. She felt his arm brush hers and she bit her tongue until she tasted blood.

Her mother arrived with a tray with two mugs of hot chocolate and a large chocolate chip scone. Val's heart sank. "Okay, guys, here you are!"

How romantic. All we need now are rose petals and candlelight.

Having claimed a small table in the back, Mom ushered them over to it. John went obediently, as if he didn't have a care in the world, moving gracefully around the throng of people. Dragging her feet as if she were being led to the guillotine, Val followed, trying again to deter her mother. She was alarmed when her voice came out in shaky syllables.

"Mom, I don't really—"

"Sure, you do," John said suddenly, giving her a look that was so direct, her words dried up in her throat like a piece of paper on fire.

Her mouth moved soundlessly as he reached out his hand towards her. She couldn't stop herself from flinching.

His jaw tightened as he put his hand on her shoulder and pushed her firmly into a chair. He started to sit across from her when he stopped, looking speculative. "On second thought, let me sit there."

She blinked up at him. "What?"

"Let me sit facing the door." His voice was nearly lost in the noise of the bakery.

"Why—"

"John, you are such a good guy to have around. I swear I should hire you to be my daughters' bodyguard." Her mother smiled. "Val, come on, move."

John chuckled. "Just keeping an eye out, Mrs. D. No big deal."

Face flaming red, Val got up and slinked into the other seat as her mother set the tray of goodies on the table. She perched on the edge of her chair, stiff and uncomfortable. John folded himself into the chair across from her.

Mom beamed at them. "Okay, I've got to go. See you guys later."

She gave Val a quick kiss and a wink that made her blush even deeper. Then she patted John on the shoulder and walked away. He smiled after her, and Val tried not to notice the dimple in his cheek or the way his straight teeth cut a nice white path across his bronzed face.

Now left alone, well, as alone as they could get with a bakery hopping full of customers, Val could only sit cemented in place, too afraid to move or even breathe. She blinked hard, staring down at the scone in front of her and the steam that rose languidly from the hot chocolate. Her stomach rumbled unpleasantly. She barely kept her butt in her seat when John shifted forward, resting his elbows on the table. The table was hardly big enough for one person let alone two and she could swear she could feel every exhale of his breath.

This is the part where he kills me, she thought, panicking. *Okay, well, maybe not kill. Maybe maim because this is my mom's bakery and I don't think he'd be so cruel as to make my own mother witness my grisly demise amongst the muffins.*

Her brain was going deaf from all the screaming it was doing. Screaming at her to get up, to move, to run, to take action because if she sat here another second longer, *she* was going to scream. But she felt frozen in place, her turbulent thoughts feeding her anxiety and immobility. She couldn't really believe that he *wanted* to sit across from her and split a chocolate chip scone. She couldn't believe that he wanted to walk her home. Or maybe he just volunteered so he could get her alone and rip her a new one. That made the most sense and she would deserve it.

God, would she deserve it.

She tried not to think about how frail he looked in the hospital. She tried not to think about their conversation in the bookstore, his unshakeable loyalty and strength and how, like a fool, she'd run from it. With his willingness to throw himself headfirst into a fight without even knowing the details but only knowing enough that she was in danger, to protect her without hesitation, it was no wonder he was such close friends with Sam. She had protected Val and the rest of their family and it was just as self-sacrificing and just as dangerous, if not more so.

Sadness overwhelmed her panic. Not only was she an idiot. She was a *blind* idiot. She was pulled away from her disparaging thoughts when John placed one of the mugs of hot chocolate in front of her. Steam swirled up, curling and twisting, doing its best to put her at ease. But that wasn't going to happen, not with John staring at her from less than two feet away.

"It's going to get cold," he mumbled at her when she made no move to pick up the cup.

"I—I can take it home and heat it up," she stammered out lamely.

John's clenched jaw looked ready to snap off. "So my company's not good enough for you?"

She blinked. "What?"

"Or would you rather have Jude sitting here instead of me?" His eyes were fierce, unwavering as they drilled into her head like heavy Earthmoving machines.

"I—no—" she managed, barely able to get the words out.

"You sure?"

"Y—Yeah—"

"I mean you guys are pretty close so I don't want to step on anyone's toes."

She blushed. "No, we're not—"

"No?" he asked, cutting her off again. "Really? I heard different."

She licked her lips, her gut tightening painfully. "No—"

"Yeah," he said with a careless shrug that looked stiff and not careless at all. "You were pretty cozy with him so he obviously doesn't scare you, huh? Like the way I'm scaring you right now?"

She opened her mouth to respond but nothing came out. Somewhere behind her, a dish broke. The sound was muted though, as if she were looking in through a glass window. The hustle and bustle around her continued, seeming to speed up, unmindful of her sitting there, completely powerless. She wondered if this is what it felt like to be a mannequin in a display window, locked in suspended animation; hyper-aware of the life passing by on the other side of the glass. She wanted to leap up and join that life, to blend in, to let it absorb her because it was far better than facing this fear that was borne out of guilt.

John was wrong. Jude had scared her and scared her still. He scared her with the unknown, with uncertainty, with the way he touched her so blatantly, so casually and making her feel things that were so incredibly foreign. Then only stopping when it suited his own purpose, not because of her. And as usual, the hell-spawned existence of high school twisted it into something unrecognizable and false and John, her white knight, her freaking Superman, thought that she actually *liked* being accosted in the hallway by someone who might or might not have been involved in the whole mess?

The annoyance that burned through her was surprising. Seriously, she got enough crap from everybody at school with their speculations and their rumors and their laughing and sneering about things that they didn't understand. She didn't need it from John. Didn't anyone know her? Didn't anyone suspect at least for a moment that there might've been some slight exaggeration about this "make-out session?" Judging by everyone's reaction and presently the look on John's face, the answer was a big, fat *hell no*.

She pressed her lips together and forced herself to make eye contact and keep it. She nearly buckled beneath the full weight of his glare but she held firm, folding her hands in front of her so tightly, her knuckles went white.

"Since when do you believe everything you hear?" she snapped.

He didn't answer which she'd assumed he wouldn't, but the hard clenching of his jaw lessened just enough to be noticeable. He curled one hand around his cup, his pale eyes never leaving her face.

"You gonna tell me otherwise?"

The challenge was in plain sight and a part of her automatically rose to meet it. But then she stopped herself and forced out a long breath, bracing herself for what was to come.

"I shouldn't have to explain myself to anyone."

He tilted his head slightly to one side. "You don't think you owe me that?"

She sat back and raked her hands through her hair. "I thought I was doing everyone a favor."

"By what? Keeping quiet?"

"I figured the less you knew, the safer you'd be."

He let out a small humorless laugh and waved a hand towards his face. "Yeah and look how well that turned out."

"I was scared," she said, hunching forward, her voice squeezed down low and hoarse as emotions began to boil beneath the surface.

"Of what? Jude?"

She shook her head with a grunt of aggravation. "What do you want to know, John? Why don't you just come right out and ask me?"

He moved suddenly, grabbing her chair and dragging it around the table. Her knee crashed into the table legs, her sneaker hit the foot of the table, rocking the whole thing haphazardly. She grabbed at it, trying to steady it.

"John!" she gasped, startled. "What're you doing?"

The hot chocolate sloshed dangerously in the cups and the scone slid across the plate, making a beeline for the edge of the table but John stopped it with a sharp slap of his palm. He finished jerking her chair up to his, eyeballing her from mere inches away now. She gaped at him. Several customers had turned to watch the commotion. John paid them no mind but Val flushed scarlet with embarrassment.

"My mother works here," she hissed. "Do you think you can keep the crazy down to a dull roar?"

"Would you even tell me if I asked you?" he practically snarled, his voice hard like gravel. "Or you gonna keep it a secret like everything else?"

"I did *not* keep anything a secret—" she automatically rebutted even though she knew it was true.

"Yes, you were," he cut in and gone was his usual mask of calm.

In its place was more emotion, more fire than she'd ever seen on his face, even more when he was in the middle of a fight. His eyes snapped with green lightening and there was a slight tinge of red to his cheeks. The veins stood out against the smooth flesh of his throat.

This was the core of him, she realized and she thought it resembled a sleeping volcano.

All quiet on the outside but rumbling and burning at the center.

It stole her breath for a moment and she could tell that it pissed him off that he was showing this side of himself to her. John was a guy who played with his cards close to his chest. He never showed them to anyone; not unless he had to and even then, he might not. Val wasn't sure if she should feel honored or terrified.

"Okay," she relented after a hesitant pause. "Okay, I did keep it a secret but I had a good reason."

"Then by all means, why don't you share it with the rest of the class?"

She bristled at his tone. "You know—"

"Sam is one of my best friends, Val," he said, his eyes burning into hers. "You know that. Hell, everyone knows that. Whatever's going on, I can help you. You know that, too. Why wouldn't you tell me? Why the hell did you think you could do this by yourself? I mean, Audrey and Bryan are about two steps away from kicking your ass up to your back teeth."

"What're they waiting for?"

"I told them I wanted to talk to you first. I told them I wanted to see if I could help straighten this out before they put you back in the hospital."

"You did help me, John, remember? And *you* were the one who ended up in the hospital *with a concussion.*"

"That doesn't matter."

"Yes, it does. It would've been a lot worse if I *had* told you."

He shook his head. "I'd do it again in a heartbeat, whether you'd told me anything or not."

"You would've ended up dead!" she exclaimed then blushed when her words attracted attention.

He gave her a look. "Are you serious?"

"Yes. You have no idea who's involved."

"Who? That scrawny little punk from the mall? Please, girl, I can take him with my eyes closed."

She shook her head, frustrated. "I wish I had your confidence."

"You should have more confidence *in me.*"

"Confidence doesn't mean anything if you're dead."

"Why do you keep saying that?"

"Because it's true. My life was threatened. Sam's life was threatened. Your little vacation in the hospital was a warning, John."

"A warning that could've been prevented had you only spoken up."

She groaned and dropped her face into her hand. "I know. God, I know." She looked at him imploringly.

"Look, I'm sorry, all right? I'm sorry I didn't tell you. I'm sorry you ended up in the hospital. I never meant for any of this to happen, least of all to you."

He was silent for a moment, his eyes searching her face.

"Tell me."

"John—"

"*Tell me.*"

It was as close to begging as she would probably ever get from him. She sighed.

And told him what she could.

He never once looked away from her. She chose her words carefully, telling him just enough to reveal Sam's involvement with Ed but not *how* she was involved with him. She told him about her run-in with Jude, tried not to shy away from the sudden hot pulse of anger that came from him.

Geez, calm down, she wanted to tell him. *Nothing happened.*

But something almost *did* happen, and she almost couldn't blame him for being mad. Then a thought stopped her.

Why exactly was he so mad about the whole Jude thing anyway?

She couldn't dwell on it because John was asking her, "What was inside the book?"

"I don't know."

He pressed his lips in a tight line, watching her. "What do you *think* was in that book?"

"John, I can't even hazard a guess—"

"You're not telling me everything."

"John, come *on*—"

He twisted around his seat so he faced her head on. He laid one arm across the back of her chair and the other arm on the table in front of her, caging her in. If she thought her heart was pounding hard before; now it was damn near painful.

"Valerie, just tell me. You already told the cops—"

"I told the cops everything that I just told you."

"Then you didn't tell them everything either."

Val bit the inside of her lip until she tasted blood. "Yes, I did."

"You're a bad liar."

She slammed her fist down on the table, startling both of them. "You don't know anything about me."

He leaned into her until she could feel his breath on her face. "Are you kidding me, Valerie? I've known you for about as long as I've known Sam. I know everything about you, probably more than you know about me."

"Congratulations," she shot back. "You're Mr. Mysterious. If you want to find out so badly, why don't you just ask Sam?"

"Because she's giving me the same bullshit that you are."

"Well then, don't you think that there might be a reason for that?"

"No reason that's good enough."

She moved her head back, glaring at him so hard she was beginning to give herself a headache. "How's the view from where you're sitting, John? Is it nice and comfy? It's pretty easy to judge from where you're at, isn't it?" She leaned into his face this time. "Do you even want to contemplate what would happen if everything was brought out into the open?"

His lips twitched. "What else is there when you claim you've told me and the cops everything already?"

"You did say I was a bad liar."

"You are."

"Okay, fine, so you know there's more than what I'm telling you."

"Yeah."

"Good. Then know this too, because I'm never going to repeat it. If you ever find out all the details, it won't be from me. It'll be from someone who wants you to know, and that someone is not me."

He looked at her as if she were a difficult math problem. "You don't want to tell me? Even though you know I'll help you? Valerie, geez, I'll protect you. You and Sam, whatever it takes."

She stared at him, suddenly wanting to hug him. He seemed so confused, so uncertain at her refusal to accept anything he had to offer. It was another look she'd never seen on him before. It was kind of nice to see that he was as human as everybody else, that he didn't have an answer to everything and that there were some things that even he couldn't do.

She pushed away from the table and stood up. He frowned.

"Val…"

She walked away from him and whereas she could've very easily spilled everything to him, she knew she was doing the right thing. He'd already been hurt because of this. She doubted that even Sam would want him to get in the line of fire.

"Valerie!"

Ignoring him, she pushed through the crowd of people and left the bakery.

CHAPTER 24

Of course, thinking that she could leave him behind in the bakery was ridiculous. He followed her outside, calling her name repeatedly until she finally stopped and turned around.

"*What*, for God's sakes?"

He stopped a foot away from her. For a moment, he didn't move, didn't speak. Then he slid his hands into his pockets. Something seemed to settle in his eyes.

"You're not supposed to walk home by yourself."

Surprised, she blinked at him then let out a tired laugh. "Right," she said.

Movement behind him caught her eye. Something quick and darting like a squirrel, moving in and out of the crowds of people on the sidewalk. Frowning, she leaned to one side, trying to see around John's bulky frame. John frowned as well and turned just in time for someone to pop up right in front of him. Val's entire body jumped as if shocked through with electricity.

Ed's angry face was split with a demonic smile and there was barely time to draw a breath before he smashed his fist into John's face. Blood flew from his mouth as John hit the ground. Letting out a startled scream, she stumbled back. Ed came towards her, his hands curled into hooks as if he were going to tear her apart. His dark eyes flashed with barely-repressed rage, churning and crackling. His handsome face twisted into something deadly and cold and looking into it, Val felt real fear.

"You bitch," he spat, his words shaking with the force of his rage. "You fucking bitch. Are you kidding me? You're gonna have me arrested? You have any idea who the fuck I am?"

She shook her head, her voice failing her. She backed away from him, her eyes flicking to John who was on the ground, holding his hands to his face, blood pouring from between his fingers.

"You are fucking dead. You, your sister, that little bastard brother of yours, you're all dead. You think you can fuck with me, fuck with my business." He let out a laugh that was callous and hard. "I am going to take you apart."

"Run, Val!" John suddenly shouted. "Run!"

Ed laughed again, a ripple traveling down the corded muscles of his arms. "Yeah, run, Val. Come on. Make me work for it. Come on."

"Val!"

She had a glimpse of John's bloodied mouth, then turned and tore down the street. Ed's laughter followed her, snapping at her heels like demon dogs.

"Yeah, go on, Val!" he shouted after her, laughing manically. "Go on, run! Go faster, come on, stretch those legs! You play ball, don't you? Come on, I'm catching up to you! I'm catching up to you, Val!"

Tears blurred her eyes, his voice making her ears hurt. Her thoughts were a screaming jumble, the world a distorted kaleidoscope as she ran faster, faster, oh God, please, faster...

"Val!" Ed screamed from behind her. Jesus was that his fingers brushing, grabbing at her hair?

A sound that was half-sob, half-scream tore from her throat. Her lungs burned with the desire for air that was caught somewhere in the vicinity of her chest. She could almost hear his pounding footsteps on the concrete behind her.

Close...so close...

"Gonna kill you...gonna gut you open, I swear to God..." His words were hissed like steam, an enraged monologue of what he was going to do to her when he got his hands on her. And Sam.

Sam!

She was coming down the steps of their apartment building with her dad and Justin. Hysterically, Val thought of the doctor's appointment he was taking her to and *hey everyone, look who's coming to dinner?*

She tried to scream out a warning as she barreled towards them. The words were locked in her throat. She could feel tears dripping down her face, saliva pooling in her mouth and there was death at her back and she couldn't even shout a warning. She sucked in a deep breath that nearly gagged her.

"Sam!" she screamed. The word exploded out of her. Her ears popped. "Dad!"

They turned, saw her tearing down the block towards them, saw them freeze in their tracks. Frantically, Val waved at them.

"Get back!" she shouted, her voice breaking at the end. "Get back inside!"

Her father tossed the keys to Sam then ran towards Val as if his hair was on fire. Val had never seen her father run before, and she couldn't believe how fast he was moving. But what was he *doing*?

"Dad!" she shrieked. "Dad, get back inside, what're you doing?"

As he raced past her, she saw his eyes, wild and full of things that she couldn't even comprehend. Distinctly, she heard the collision of two human bodies. She slowed and turned around to find her father grappling with Ed on the sidewalk. They rolled and pulled. Ed tried to punch him but he couldn't get leverage.

"Dad!"

"Go, Val!" he shouted at her from over his shoulder. "Go now! Call the police!"

"Get the fuck off me, man!" Ed snarled, his legs kicking.

Sam was suddenly beside her, her eyes wide and frightened. She pulled on Val's arm.

"Come on. Val, come on," she said desperately.

Val followed her and Justin up the stairs but before they could go inside the building, a sharp cry came from behind them.

"Dad!" Justin cried, his face pale and trembling.

Val saw her father lying on the ground, cradling his face.

And Ed...

Ed was already on his feet and coming towards them.

"Come on, get inside, Val, *Val*, move your ass!" Sam shouted in her ear.

"Go!" Dad shouted, trying to stand. "Go!"

They ran into the building, hitting the stairs at a frantic pace.

"Come on!" Sam shouted again.

She kept a hand on Justin's arm, half-dragging, half-carrying him but his foot caught on the step and he went sprawling. Val lurched to the side, nearly topping over him.

"Justin!" she gasped. "Come on, buddy, get up, get up!"

She tried to help him up but her hands wouldn't cooperate. He seemed to curl into the stairs, a shuddering mess of nerves and fear, sobs racking his entire body.

"Shit!" Sam swore under her breath.

She gave Val a shove up the steps. "Go!" she commanded before bending down and scooping Justin up into her arms.

He clung to her, tears glistening like diamonds on his cheeks. Val could see his face, a mask of confusion and fright, peering over Sam's shoulder, his small hands hooked into her shirt. Sam pounded up the steps, her long legs allowing her to take two at a time, bypassing Val easily. But she looked over her shoulder every time they reached a new landing, checking to see that Val was close, calling to her, urging her to *hurry*.

"Come on, come on, come on," she chanted. "Val, please, come on!"

Val tried to respond, tried to tell her that she was coming, that she was moving but her lungs were on fire. She kept her hands on the railing to pull herself along because her legs shook, wanting to stop but the rest of her refused.

She heard the front door of the building crash open and suddenly Ed was inside, coming after them, rising up from below like some devastating beast.

His screams filled the air, reverberating horribly, bouncing around them like giant razor-edged ping pong balls. The fury in his words was catastrophic and terrifying.

"Sam!" he screamed up to them. "Sam, get back here, girl and maybe I won't beat you like the dog you are!"

Val risked a glance over the railing and saw his sweaty, rage-thinned face peering back at her. He was so close, his quick, lithe movements eating up the distance between them in no time at all. His eyes were lit by a crazy light, his teeth gnashing together like a shark feeding on a whale carcass.

"Sam! You bitch! After everything I did for you? Everything I gave you, this is how you treat me? You're running from me? That's pretty unfair, you know that? But hey! It doesn't matter! I'll show you how unfair I can be!"

His words roared in Val's ears and she went sprawling as she hit the next landing.

"Val!" Sam screamed from above her.

Ed was suddenly on her, all over her as he grabbed her by the hair and yanked her to her feet.

"I'll show you what happens when girls are bad, Valerie," he spat in her face. "You hear me, Sam?" he shouted up the stairs. "I'm gonna show your little sister here everything I showed you and we'll just have to wait and see which one of you is the better—"

Val rammed her knee up between his legs. The air left him in a giant *whoosh*, his hate-filled words dying in a sound that was something like an injured cow. He curled in on himself and sank to his knees. She twisted out his grip.

"Val!" Sam cried. "Val, come on!"

She leapt up the steps, feeling Ed's fingers graze her ankle. She reached their floor and bolted down the hallway. Sam was already standing in front of their apartment, the keys slipping and sliding through her sweaty, shaking fingers. Justin was next to her now, pressed into her side, his cries soft and awful.

"Sam!" Val shouted. "Sam, come on, unlock the door!"

"What the hell do you think I'm trying to do?"

The keys fell from her hands. She snatched them up. Val skidded to a stop beside her, casting glances over her shoulder. Panic was a sharp-taloned beast in the back of her throat. She went to Justin, pulling him against her.

"Is that him?" he sobbed. "Is that him, Val?"

Sam looked down at him then at Val. Val met her eyes and swallowed hard. "Yeah. Yeah, that's him," she replied, her voice catching as a sob escaped.

Sam squeezed her eyes shut then opened them. Her chest heaved as she tried to catch her breath.

"I'm sorry," she whispered. "God, I'm so sorry, sorry, sorry, I'm sorry."

"*Sam!*"

They all jumped and turned to see Ed stumbling towards them, one hand cradling his groin, the other on the wall. He wasn't running, which was good but he was moving quickly, too quickly for someone who just got kicked in the family jewels.

"Sam, oh my God, open the door," Val said, her voice thick with fear.

"I know, I know, *I know.*"

"Sam! Hurry!" Justin cried desperately.

She slammed the right key into the lock, twisted it and threw the door open.

"Go, go, go, go, go!"

"Sam!" Ed shouted again and Val knew she was going to have nightmares of his screams for months.

They piled in then slammed the door shut as his enraged face came into view, his anger, his ferocity filling the doorway like a cloud of thick, black smoke. The locks were thrown into place and as one, Val, Sam and Justin huddled together and moved away from the door. Ed pounded madly on it from the other side, his curses filtering through, the door groaning in protest at the abuse. The madness reached for them and they backed away until they stood in the kitchen, trembling and gasping for breath.

"Open this fucking door!" he ranted. "God help you, Sam, you better open this door! If you're smart, you'll do it, Sam. I might decide not to kill you, who knows? I told you what would happen if you went to the police so come out here like a good girl and face your punishment!"

Suddenly there was the sound of running feet, a horde of running feet, shouts, breathless grunts, followed by, "Hey, get off me, this is harassment!"

Something heavy hit the floor and there were sounds of a struggle. Val stared at the door, trying to blink away the tears from her eyes but they kept refilling. Sam's arm was nearly a noose around her neck and Justin was a solid weight against her side. It was the closest they'd ever been without complaining.

Muffled words and panting, painful and desperate seemed to come from the crack beneath the door like something was trying to worm its way in. Then, "Sam?"

Sam gasped, cringing. Val's arms shook, fingers biting into Sam's shoulder. Justin hiccupped against her stomach.

"Val? Justin? Hey guys, it's me. Open the door, okay?"

"Dad," Sam whispered.

"Dad?" Justin called out tentatively.

"It's me, guys."

Just as before when they moved away from the door holding onto each other, they moved towards it, without letting go. With trembling fingers, Val unlocked the door and opened it carefully to find chaos in the hallway. Police officers were everywhere and Ed was being led away, still screaming and in handcuffs.

"Oh my God! Oh God!" Dad cried softly, barreling into them, wrapping them all up in his arms, his body quaking with relief. Justin curled into his legs while Sam and Val each took a shoulder, falling against him in relief and tears.

"Oh my God," he whispered again, pressing hard kisses on Val's forehead before doing the same to Sam. He stroked an unsteady hand through Justin's hair. "Oh, my babies, are you all right? Huh? You okay?"

Val pressed her face into his shoulder before looking up at him. She winced when she saw the bruise on his cheek.

"It's all right," he said softly. "It's okay."

She hugged him. Sam sobbed quietly into his shoulder. Dad shushed her.

"It's all right, Sam. We're okay now. See? All in one piece."

She gave a weak nod. After a moment, she moved her head back so she could see him.

"Dad, I need to tell you what was in the book that Val gave to the police."

CHAPTER 25

Human trafficking.

The fact that it had a name made it even more shocking. The Delton family sat in the cold gray interview room of the police station, listening silently in horror as Detective Allen backed up what Sam had told them. The book lay in the center of the table like a dead fish, a catalyst for all their sorrow. Val wanted nothing more than to watch it be reduced to a pile of ashes and then scattered.

Ed, all twenty-two years of him, had been a human trafficker, a sex slave driver, a pimp for nearly three years. He got into the game by drugging his then-girlfriend, Lindsay, and allowing three friends to have sex with her while she lay passed out on the couch. That night, he'd made his first three-hundred-dollar score and after that, he was hooked.

Realizing how much money could be made, he began recruiting girls, seventeen years old and younger. The recruitment was not unlike military officers scoping out a graduating high school class, looking for fresh young men and women to enlist, promising them all types of prestige, money, and job opportunities.

But that was where the similarities ended.

Ed showered the girls with clothes, money, endless attention, and adoration, earning their trust little by little until finally they did everything he asked with no hesitation. When it became clear what his intentions were, it was already too late. Intimidation was cruical in keeping the girls in check, in keeping them working for him. To make sure they didn't tell anyone, threats were issued on their lives and the lives of their families, constantly reinforced with beatings and bruises in areas that could easily be hidden by clothing so family and friends wouldn't get suspicious.

The book that Val had given the police had every name of every girl Ed had ever used. It held appointments, dates, parties, and names of those who didn't have a problem having unprotected sex with a fifteen-year-old girl. The book was a roadmap and its end destination was a six by six jail cell. Val wondered how often Brandon's name appeared inside that book. She was pretty sure his wasn't the only name she would recognize.

Sam sat stone-faced as Detective Allen went over everything. Every now and then, a tear would escape from the corner of her eye. If it wasn't for the white-knuckled grip she had on her mother's hand, Val would think that as usual Sam wasn't at all affected by what was going on. She allowed pictures to be taken of the cut on her collarbone, the bruises that Val hadn't seen that littered her torso, some dark and recent, others faded and yellow. She didn't even hesitate when asked if she would testify against Ed in court. There was talk about getting other girls to testify against him as well. If they were too afraid, Sam volunteered to talk to them. There was steel in her eyes now, a determination that said that Ed was never going to be a free man, as long as she still had air in her lungs.

Since Sam and Val were both under-aged, their names would not be released to the press. It was a big relief, but Sam had shocked them all by saying that one day, she was going to tell this story. She was going to let everyone know the dangers of trusting someone who says they can give you the world, the dangers of not going for help when you needed it most, the dangers of being disconnected from your family and most importantly, the dangers of not having any hope.

Later on, when they were finally home and exhaustion had settled over everyone, Val cried herself to sleep. She didn't know if it was tears of relief or sadness or maybe a mixture of both. What she did know was that things within her family were never going to be the same. Maybe that was good. Maybe that was bad. She could only hope that they would be able to heal together, as a family.

In the morning, for the first time in a long time, there was laughter in the kitchen. Val walked in, sleepy eyed and confused as she saw Justin standing on his chair with his cereal bowl on his head and a cardboard paper towel roll in his hand. He wielded it while making the weird light saber noises from *Star Wars*.

"Even Luke Skywalker wants Lucky Charms," Sam was saying as she shook the box at him.

"Never! Luke Skywalker needs Yoda, not Lucky Charms!" Justin crowed.

"Didn't Yoda like breakfast?" Dad asked.

"I never saw him eat anything," Mom chimed in.

"Yoda doesn't need to eat!" Justin exclaimed.

Sam rolled her eyes. "Oh right, he has the *force* to keep him full."

Justin vaulted off the chair, raising his cardboard sword above his head. "You mock the force?"

"Oh, I mock the force!"

He tackled her.

Val rubbed at her eyes. "It is way too early for this."

The phone rang. Sam grabbed for it but Val was closer. Sam stuck her tongue out at her as Val snickered.

"Hello?"

"Valerie."

Her heart stopped and she felt like she was suddenly encased in ice. She looked up to find everyone staring at her.

Mom frowned. "Who is it?"

Val shook her head and held up a finger. Sam looked stricken and Justin looked as if he wished the sword in his hand was real. Her father watched her carefully.

"Heard you had an exciting day yesterday," Jude said and she could see the smile that went with his words.

Val cleared her throat. "Yeah, exciting. That's one way of putting it."

He chuckled but it didn't sound like he was amused. He sounded almost...relieved. "Is everything squared away?"

"What do you mean?"

"You know, with the cops and everything? Do your parents know the whole story?"

Val wet her lips. "The cops loved that book. It's going to help a lot and yes, my parents know the whole story."

"Oh, so Sam told them?"

"Yes."

"Everything?"

"Everything."

There was silence for a minute. "I'm impressed."

"Why?"

"I wasn't expecting the whole truth to come out."

"With all the girls named in that book, it was the right thing to do. Even Sam knew that."

Sam glared at her but there was no heat behind it. Val took a deep breath. "Look, I—"

"Oh, no, no, no, don't get sappy on me now, Valerie. Come on. Don't ruin this nice image I have of you."

"And what image is that?"

"Joan of Arc."

Val let out a surprised chuckle. "That's a little—"

"Joan of Arc was fearless, Valerie. Like you. I wish my sister could've had your strength."

Val frowned. "Your sist—" she stopped, her eyes widening.

Jude's sister.

Lindsay.

"Oh my God," she whispered.

When Jude spoke again, his voice was strained like he was having a hard time getting the words out.

"Lindsay was Ed's girlfriend. The one who while passed out on the couch, thanks to the drugs Ed put in her drink, unknowingly helped him realize he could do this kind of thing for a living."

Val ran a hand through her hair, completely floored. "Is she—I mean, was she—"

"She's got her good days and bad days."

Val rested her head against the wall.

"So I have you to thank, Valerie," Jude went on.

"Me? No, you were the one who—"

"But you pursued it, Valerie. Like I said before. Fearless."

He hung up.

She stared at the phone then slowly hung it up.

"Jesus Christ, what the hell was that all about?" her father bellowed.

"Who was it? Val, who was on the phone?" Sam demanded.

Val gave a shake of her head. "Jude. It was Jude."

"What did he want?" Mom asked.

Val told them.

CHAPTER 26

"Val! Hey, how about that exclusive?" Kenny grinned as he bumped into her in the hallway after school.

"What exclusive?" she asked.

"About you and Jude, of course."

"Oh, dude, that's so old news. Don't you have anything new?"

"It's popular demand, Val. Who am I to deny the people what they want?"

"I don't think the people really care, and it's doubtful that they even believe it."

"What?" he exclaimed. "Wait, who says they don't believe—hey, Allison! Do you believe that Jude and our pal, Val here were sucking faces the other day?"

Allison gave him a look. "Are you kidding me, man?"

Kenny waved her away. "Of course, you'd say that. You're her friend."

"I don't believe it."

All three of them turned to find John standing next to Kenny, looking as unobtrusive and silent as ever. Allison's eyes widened comically as she looked at him then at Val.

Kenny stammered for a coherent sentence.

"Oh...oh, well, yeah, man, I mean, who believes this crap anyway? It's ridiculous. Really, it is. I'm sure there's more important stuff going on around here, right? Like who stole the head cheerleader's underwear? Hey, yeah! That's important, right? I'm gonna go find out more about that. See ya guys!"

He hurried off down the hallway, casting worried glances over his shoulder.

Allison's mouth flapped soundlessly then she blinked as if coming out of a trance.

"That, uh, that, yeah, what he said. Val, I'll, uh, see you later, I guess, huh?" She took off after Kenny.

"See you later," Val called after her.

Almost reluctantly, she looked up at John, wincing when she saw the fresh bruise on his jaw. It made him look dangerous, as if he wasn't dangerous already. Without thinking, she reached up for it. "I'm so sorry about this."

He caught her hand. His grip was warm and soft, sending a flush up her arm and into her face.

"It's all right," he shrugged. "It was worth it."

She sighed. "Why do you keep saying that? Getting punched in the face is so not worth it. For anyone or anything."

He smiled faintly. He still hadn't let go of her hand. His thumb moved back and forth, caressing her knuckles.

Her mouth went dry as he stared down at her, his green eyes as intense as they were the day she'd argued with him in the bakery.

"I'm glad you're all right," he said quietly.

Butterflies flapped madly inside her rib cage and she had to swallow twice to find her voice. "I'm glad you're all right, too."

His eyes didn't leave her face. "So I was thinking maybe we could hit the bakery again, you know, pick up where we left off."

She gaped up at him, wanting to look away to see if there was a camera around because this had to be some kind of joke. Right?

"W—where we left off wasn't very good," she stammered.

"Then we'll make it better."

Her cheeks burned and something like hope rose in her chest. "I...I..."

"Valerie," he murmured gently. "When are you going to stop running away from me?"

He threaded his fingers through hers. His hand was fever-warm and softer than she imagined. The blush in her face whipped down to her neck. She stared up into his eyes and saw something definitive there, something that she could never question, something that made her skin ripple with excitement. She lifted her other hand without conscious thought.

John went still as she skated her fingers, feather-light, down the uninjured side of his jaw. The hope that was rising in her chest skyrocketed to rock-hard certainty, but if she wasn't standing here, touching him, actually touching him, she never would've believed it. The smile that bloomed on her face when he leaned into her touch was so wide it almost hurt.

"Now," she said. "Right now."

THE END

About the Author

Melissa Groeling graduated from Bloomsburg University with a degree in English. She lives, reads and writes in the Philadelphia region and wherever else life happens to send her. She is a hardcore New York Giants fan and loves chocolate. *Traffic Jam* is her first young adult novel.

Made in the USA
Lexington, KY
06 June 2012